"I KNOW WHO YOU ARE, GREAT WIND-WOLF," the Indian girl said positively, her eyes shining with a strange light. "I saw you come to save me. You killed them, tore them to pieces as if they were nothing, and later when you were gone, I heard your howl."

Yes, Ruff had heard that howl too. Before he could deny being the Windwolf, the girl was in his arms, holding him tightly.

"Is it permitted to touch you?" she asked.

Ruff smiled and wiped back a lock of black hair from her too-serious brow. "It is permitted," he replied.

"Then," she said, smiling, "since you have taken the form of a man, you must have a man's comfort. . . ."

Ø

Wild Westerns From SIGNET

RUFF JUSTICE #9

WINDWOLF

By

Warren T. Longtree

A SIGNET BOOK

NEW AMERICAN LIBRARY

TIMES MIRROR

PUBLISHER'S NOTE

This novel is a work of fiction. Names, characters, places, and incidents are either the product of the author's imagination or are used fictitiously, and any resemblance to actual persons, living or dead, events, or locales is entirely coincidental.

NAL BOOKS ARE AVAILABLE AT QUANTITY DISCOUNTS WHEN USED TO PROMOTE PRODUCTS OR SERVICES. FOR INFORMATION PLEASE WRITE TO PREMIUM MARKETING DIVISION, THE NEW AMERICAN LIBRARY, INC., 1633 BROADWAY, NEW YORK, NEW YORK 10019.

The first chapter of this book appeared in *The Death of Iron Horse*, the eighth volume of this series.

SIGNET TRADEMARK REG. U.S. PAT. OFF. AND FOREIGN COUNTRIES
REGISTERED TRADEMARK—MARCA REGISTRADA
HECHO EN CHICAGO, U.S.A.

SIGNET, SIGNET CLASSICS, MENTOR, PLUME, MERIDIAN AND NAL BOOKS are published by The New American Library, Inc., 1633 Broadway, New York, New York 10019

First Printing, May, 1983

1 2 3 4 5 6 7 8 9

PRINTED IN THE UNITED STATES OF AMERICA

RUFF JUSTICE

He knew the West better than any man alive—a hostile, savage land rife with both violent outlaws and courageous adventurers. But Ruff Justice had a sixth sense that kept him breathing and saw his enemies dead. A scout for the U.S. Calvary, he was paid to protect the public, and nobody was faster at sniffing out a killer, a crook, a con man—red or white, at close range or far. Anyone on the wrong side of the law would have to reckon with the menace of Ruff's murderously sharp stag-handled bowie knife, with his Colt pistol, and the Spencer rifle he cradled in his arms.

Ruff Justice, gentleman and frontier philosopher—good men respected him, bad men feared him, and women, good and bad, wanted him with all the wildness of the Old West.

1

It was still snowing in Denver. T. Russell Hicks sat at the front window of the Imperial Hotel, a place altogether too grand and definitely too expensive for T. Russell, who had been a trapper, gun runner, teamster, whiskey trader, smuggler, and highwayman in turn, making a success of himself at none of these varied occupations.

But, he decided, he was a hell of a good drinker, one of the best. Maybe in Denver's top three. He saluted his prowess with another whiskey.

He sighed heavily.

It was late. The Imperial Band had left the stage two hours ago. The time was exact. T. Russell had been staring that long at the walnut-cased clock hanging on the wall between the two blue-paned windows which separated him from the chilling wind, the snow that fell steadily outside.

He wiped away a circle of moisture and stared out at the street, noticing that the traffic was nil. The horse trolley which ran up Grand Avenue had gone out of service because of the snow. There was one hardy or drunken cowhand jack-rabbiting his pony through the drifts, but aside from that Denver was white-shrouded, silent, empty.

Outside the window.

Inside, the saloon of the Imperial Hotel was still active. Fine ladies in their ball gowns, crusty mustached gentlemen with expensive, impressive bay windows crossed by gold chains. And that interminable voice!

T. Russell Hicks sighed one last time, started in lovingly on his beer chaser, and turned his bleary eyes again toward the stage, where a tall man in a dark suit and ruffled shirt held forth.

He was on the forty-third line of what seemed to be an endless poem in an endless string of poems. There had been a fifteen-minute pause while the people of Denver were lectured on their lack of culture—this when a weary miner tried to sneak out the side door and was brought back at gunpoint by the mustached poet.

"He's got to be drunk," the man on Hicks's right said to a table companion.

"I've been watching him," the other man answered. "He hasn't had a drink all night."

"Well then, he's plain damn crazy," the first man huffed. "I'd leave, but I don't want him drawing that revolver again."

To Hicks's left an overaged debutante sighed, "Isn't he beautiful?" Hicks's answer was to call for another round of drinks.

"It was only a soddy on Cottonwood Creek,
A place where Ken Crowder hid out for a
    week,
While the posse trailed phantoms and
    shades . . ."

2

Hicks downed another shot, hoping that they hanged the outlaw sometime in the next hundred lines. It wasn't to be.

"Who *is* he?" the debutante asked, holding her hand to her bosom. "What a magnificent animal."

Ken Crowder was still holding off the posse:

"He leaped from his horse and his six-guns
    they barked
His silver spurs flashed, he escaped in the dark
To fight one more day for his freedom."

"Why, dear, I thought everyone knew. That's Ruff Justice."

It was indeed. Amusement danced in Justice's blue eyes as he stalked upstage and down, hands behind his back, reciting *The Ballad of a Good Man Gone Bad.* Men shuffled their feet and started to nod off. Women sat with their eyes sparkling, enraptured.

He was tall. His dark hair was worn long, curling down across his shoulders. A matching black mustache drooped to his jawline. He was known across the West as the "poet scout," and his scouting was generally acknowledged as top-flight. There had been some dissent about the quality of the poetry. Generally these dissenters voiced their opinions out of Justice's earshot.

"And they hung him from the tall lonesome
    pine."

"Should hang Ruff Justice too," someone grumbled. He was a Denver miner with plenty of serious drinking to do. He had been sitting for two hours listening to this crazy man spout poetry.

Much of it didn't even rhyme. When someone in the crowd had pointed that out, Justice, breaking off in mid-stanza, had come forward and dragged the man up on stage, insisting that he come up with a better rhyme.

The trouble was, the miner decided, you couldn't judge if the man was serious or was subjecting them all to this for his own entertainment. One thing he was sure of. That was a tough man. It was in his icy blue eyes. You could read it there: much hard weather, a lot of hard miles, and perhaps much blood.

There was a smattering of applause—it seemed to be only the women who were clapping. Ruff Justice stepped forward and peered at his audience across the footlights.

"If you don't like that one, I do have another prepared."

That brought them all to their feet applauding, and Justice, with a little nod, turned and walked from the stage. T. Russell Hicks finished his last shot of whiskey and followed unsteadily, heading for the corridor behind the backstage area.

"Wonderful," Belinda said, and she pressed her lips to Ruff's.

"Was it?"

"You. You're wonderful." Belinda smiled.

They stood backstage among the scenery from forgotten plays, the sawdust smell surrounding them, Belinda's arms around Ruff's neck.

She was not yet twenty. Her gown showed her full, firm breasts to good advantage. Her eyes fixed on those of Ruff Justice.

"Why do you do that to them?" she asked impishly.

"It's a matter of bringing culture to the city of Denver," Justice said without cracking a smile.

She stepped back, her hands still resting on his shoulders, her eyes running up and down the tall man. She squeezed him tightly again, and she whispered, her breath warm and moist against his neck, "Bring a little culture to me, Mr. Justice."

"Here?" Ruff looked around at the dark storeroom. Onstage a soprano was experimenting to see if a high A could pop a corset.

"Why not?"

Ruff nodded and led her slowly back toward a pile of old stage curtains, managing to shed his coat as he did so. At his waist was a Colt New Line Pocket .41, Ruff Justice's town gun. Belinda's eyes weren't on the gun.

She got to her knees and began fussing with Justice's trousers, and some very nice fussing it was. Her fingers undid his belt and unbuttoned his pants.

She paused a minute, her cheek against his leg. Then, smiling, she came to her feet, undoing all sorts of clasps and gewgaws until her dress, followed by petticoats and chemise, fell away, and Belinda, not waiting to unbutton her shoes, sank onto the pile of curtains in the dark corner of the backstage storeroom.

The lady on stage continued to weave her way through the operatic solo as Ruff went to Belinda, his hand running over her body, up along her sleek, long thigh to her hip, across her flat abdomen to briefly cup her full breast before it returned to nestle into the soft, flourishing bush between her legs.

"I don't want to wait," Belinda said, the words breathy and constricted. "Not sure I can."

Ruff rolled to her and she grabbed at him, positioning him as he fitted himself to her, feeling her warmth surround him, feeling her heated breath on his cheek, the warm, hungry ministrations of her lips.

Belinda's head fell back and her hips began to thrust and roll as her fingers tightened on Ruff's shoulders. Her eyes were sparkling, distant, as their bodies tangled themselves together.

Belinda cried out softly and bit at her knuckle to quiet her exclamation of joy. The man above her worked patiently, intently, bringing her to a peak of sensation, and she cried out again, her shriek blending with the second attempt at a high A from the soprano. Belinda laughed. She laughed even as Justice brought her to a second crest of sensation, and her body shook with ecstasy and laughter.

"Your note was much better," Ruff whispered into her ear, and she laughed harder. Momentarily.

Then the feeling became so intense as wave after wave of pleasure swept over her that there was no laughter, no speech, no world, only the long man with the dark hair, only his constant, deliberate, maddening lovemaking, until she thought that she would burst open with the joy of it.

Only then did Justice allow himself to reach his own completion, and Belinda lay back, feeling a tear run hotly across her cheek, a tear for which there was no explanation, and Ruff Justice kissed it away.

"A performance . . ." she panted and looked at him, touching his lips with her fingertip. "That on the stage was nothing. This is your greatest performance."

6

The soprano reached a last wilted, quavering note, and lukewarm applause sounded through the hall.

"Do you think they liked her better?" he asked, kissing Belinda's small, round ear.

"I wouldn't," she said, snuggling up to him. "Would you?"

"Maybe she would take her shoes off," Ruff said. "I've got some unusual bruises." Belinda laughed once more, softly, and Ruff kissed her deeply, feeling her searching lips, her darting tongue, meet his own.

He lay in her arms, feeling the gentle pulsings of their quieting bodies, lounging in the warmth of her, and thinking as he looked toward the curtains which separated them from the stage what sort of appreciation the people of Denver might demonstrate for this sort of show.

Suddenly he came alert. He dropped his hand to the pile of clothing at his side and slipped the little .41 from its holster.

"What is . . . ?"

"Ssh!" Ruff put a finger to her lips. He frowned.

He had heard something. Another unappreciative audience going to have a try at hanging him? Ruff smiled thinly and silently drew back the hammer of the Colt.

Belinda's eyes were wide, frightened. Ruff smiled and stroked her hair. Then, sliding from the love nest, he crouched, looking toward the rack of scenery flats to the right where the sound seemed to come from.

Hastily, motioning for Belinda to be silent, he covered her with the old curtains, throwing her clothing in with her.

He crossed the floor on cat feet, crouched low, the air cool against his naked body. His Colt was before him, cocked and ready. His dark hair hung in his eyes. He stopped, still in a crouch, listening.

Those ears had been conditioned to listen patiently. He had survived in wild country a good long time, depending on hearing as much as seeing. At night eyes were useless; in Indian country you never saw the hostiles until they were ready for you to see them. But there was always some sound, however slight: the whisper of brush against fabric as a hunter moved through the undergrowth, the faint, hushed scraping of a moccasin over sand.

He was hearing such sounds now, sounds which didn't belong. But the man who was making them hadn't the tenth part of an Apache's skill.

From the stage a cacophony of new sounds rose now, washing out the smaller ones backstage. A troupe of jugglers had begun their act.

It didn't matter. Ruff had found his man. The canvas scenery flats fluttered in their rack. And Ruff Justice waited, clinging to the shadows near the curtain.

His patience was rewarded.

The figure of a man appeared. He was trying his damnedest to be stealthy, but failing miserably. Still, with that pistol in his hand, he was as potentially deadly as any man who had ever walked the earth.

Ruff viewed him in that way, not feeling a bit sorry for T. Russell Hicks, who had failed at everything he had ever tried and was about to fail for the last time.

Hicks was creeping toward the pile of curtains where Belinda, still unmoving, lay. Ruff couldn't let him get there—there was no telling what would happen under such circumstances. Hicks might just decide to empty that Smith & Wesson he was carrying into the heaped curtains.

"T. Russell," Ruff said softly, disengaging from the shadows.

"Goddam," T. Russell Hicks muttered. He had blown this too. He knew Justice and he knew that he didn't have much of a chance. Through his mind flitted the desperate thought that his only chance was to fire first and trust to luck.

Luck wasn't on T. Russell Hicks's side that night any more than it had ever been.

His first shot went wild, slapping against the wall beyond Ruff Justice. The second went high into the loft, cutting loose a sandbag which counterbalanced the stage curtain. The sandbag dropped heavily to the floor, the curtain behind Ruff Justice went up; T. Russell Hicks took a soft-nosed .41 in his head and fell back, his skull pierced cleanly, his face a mask of blood.

Ruff Justice strode toward him, his gun at the ready. He suddenly became aware of the applause at his back, and he turned to find a troupe of jugglers staring at him, and across the footlights Denver's citizenry standing, peering, fainting, cheering.

Ruff realized simultaneously that he was naked, and decided that the performance should be cut short. He turned, bowed from the waist, and made his exit, followed by Belinda, who bounced up from beneath the curtains to a stormy ovation and rushed toward the wings, ending what was all in all the best performance of the night, and some said of the winter, at the Denver, Colorado, Imperial Hotel.

2

The marshal was not applauding, nor was he smiling. His name was Bartholomew Meek, hardly a fitting name. Meek was several inches over six feet tall, hawk-nosed, scar-faced, with a violent shock of red hair. His eyes were dark. They were brooding eyes, the eyes of a man who had seen too much trouble, too much blood.

Meek shifted in his chair and crossed his legs, taking a slow, deep breath. The man across the hotel room from the town marshal of Denver, Colorado, seemed completely composed, utterly relaxed. He smiled softly, not at the marshal, but at some distant thought Meek couldn't guess at.

They called him Ruff Justice. Tall, lean, he had the coldest blue eyes Meek had ever encountered. His aspect was one of competence, self-assurance, and there was a deadly subsurface current which Meek could not define. It was an invisible aura, an electrical prickling along the back of the marshal's neck. He had felt this before, in other places, facing other men, but they had inevitably been the mean ones, the killers. Justice did not fit into that category. The question was—where did he fit?

"What happened?" Meek said finally.

"Man came trying to kill me. I got him first," Justice said quietly.

"Did you know him?"

"I've run into him from time to time. T. Russell wasn't a hell of a lot of man. He'd flopped at everything and he flopped at this." Ruff smiled again. "Fortunately."

"Did he have a particular grudge against you, Mr. Justice?"

"He'd been sitting all evening listening to my poetry," Ruff told him. "Some people might say that was reason enough."

Meek ignored it; he was in no mood for humor. "Fifty gold dollars were found in Hicks's pockets. T. Russell hadn't held a job in over six months. Where do you suppose he got that money, Mr. Justice?"

"Conjecture? He got it to kill me."

"Think so?"

"Seems obvious," Ruff said.

"From who? Who wants you dead, Justice?"

"I couldn't say," Ruff answered. The eyes said that Justice wasn't telling the entire story, but Meek knew he would get nothing out of this one.

"Mind if I ask exactly what it is that brings you to Denver, Mr. Justice?"

"Visiting. I wanted to perform at the Imperial."

"That what you usually do—perform? Read poetry and such?" Meek asked with a hint of disgust.

"That's what I sometimes do," Justice answered.

"Who was the woman?"

"Which woman?"

"Which woman? Which woman do you think I'm talking about, Justice? The one who was backstage when the curtain fell. The one who sprinted off naked."

"I believe she was a stage actress."

"But you don't know." Meek's eyes narrowed. Justice wasn't going to tell him anything, he realized, but a man had to try. Justice shrugged.

"A woman."

"So you don't know why Hicks tried to kill you. You don't know who might have hired him. You don't know who the naked woman was."

Justice stood and walked to the hotel window, looking out at the muddy streets, at the purple, snow-streaked mountains beyond. For a minute he thought about telling Meek all of it. But there was no point in it, and Meek himself might be the next target.

"I've told you all I can." Justice turned his back to the window and leaned against it. Bluish light struck across his shoulders, painting patches on the wooden floor of the hotel room.

"I understand you used to work for the army. Some kind of scout back in Dakota. Why'd you leave?"

"My relationship with the army seems to get a little strained from time to time," Ruff answered. "When it gets strained enough, I leave."

"They gave you the boot," Meek suggested.

"Something like that." Ruff grinned, and Meek despite himself found that he was grinning back.

"All right, Mr. Justice," Meek said, rising, taking his hat from his knee to plant it on his head. "There's not much doubt that it was self-defense. Everyone agrees to that. They heard two shots fired before you cut loose. Two empty cartridges in his gun. Damn me if I like this solution, though. He was hired, that's obvious, and if he

12

was hired there'll be another man on his heels, likely. You've thought of that?"

"Quite frequently." And likely, Ruff thought, he would be a better man.

"It's best for everyone if you get out of Denver. That's what I'm telling you to do. Understand me?"

"I understand." Ruff looked again out the window. The skies were clear, the snow melting across the meadows. It was time to be going, time to be after his own prey.

"Good." Meek nodded, looked again at Mr. Ruffin T. Justice, shook his head, and went out, quietly closing the door to Ruff's hotel room.

Ruff's eyes followed the closing door, then swept the room. Noticing the silk stockings under the corner of the bed, he smiled. He hated to leave Denver, in a way, but an enforced idle winter had worn on him.

He had spent much time in cities, from San Francisco to Paris, the latter when he had traveled to Europe with Bill Cody in the days before Bill had begun to believe himself. He enjoyed the company of cultivated women, liked to sit down to a civilized dinner. He was at home in a ruffled shirt and suit. But he was more at home out there.

He looked beyond the window again at the wilderness landscape. Ruff threw open the window and let the cold air drift into the room. It was time to go, time to hunt, time to lay it on the line.

The job was a nasty one—but then that was the only kind he got. If it was neat and aboveboard the army took it on itself. If it was as nasty as this there was only one man for the job. Ruff Justice.

Ruff glanced in the mirror, smoothing back his

long dark hair, which just now fell across his shoulders. His mustache hung to his jawline.

"There's a savage hidden in you, Mr. Justice," he told the mirror image. There was no response from the reflection.

Thinking about the mirror, he went to his bureau, removed the daguerreotype, and returned with it. Daguerreotypes, being taken directly onto a photographic plate, always return the mirror image of the subject. Now Ruff held the faded, brown image up to the mirror and studied the face as he would see it.

A very young man with a wispy mustache and dark, lifeless eyes stared back from the looking glass. His hair was dark, smoothed down against his skull, ears small and flat, nose prominent. There was already a hint of cruelty in the face, or maybe that was imagination—knowing what had come after.

Ruff placed the daguerreotype down and studied it as he unbuttoned his white shirt. Older now, perhaps with a beard and less hair—would he recognize the man if he bumped into him?

Obviously someone thought he would, or else there was no explaining T. Russell Hicks, found dead with fifty gold dollars in his eternally empty pockets.

Ruff stripped off his shirt and tossed it onto the bed. Sitting, he started tugging at his boots, remembering the first time he had heard the name Roscoe Siringo.

"Know him?"

Colonel MacEnroe had tossed the daguerreotype across his desk, glancing at the major who sat in the far corner studying the tall man in buckskins.

Ruff Justice took the picture and studied it a minute. "No," he told the commanding officer of Fort Lincoln. "Who is he?"

"His name is Roscoe Siringo. We want you to find him."

The scout shrugged and looked again at the young major in the corner chair.

"You'd better tell me about it, colonel," Justice suggested.

MacEnroe nodded to the major, who stood, removed his hat, and come to face Ruff Justice, measuring him all the time.

"This is Major Corson from the Laramie garrison, Ruff."

Ruff inclined his head slightly. "What's it about?"

"A little background first, if I may," Corson said. He paced the room slowly as he spoke. "Roscoe Siringo was born in Virginia, moved to Plainview, Kansas, when he was three. Father a dirt farmer, not a very successful one, mother a fierce Baptist who died when Siringo was seven. Siringo was sixteen when the war broke out and had already left home under rather obscure circumstances which left his father with a gunshot wound in the leg. The old man lived only through the first year of the war.

"Siringo's life during the next five years is a mystery, although it appears now that he rode with Sangborne, a bloody guerrilla who made Quantrill look like a missionary. There's no proof of this—those units kept no records.

"Siringo was known across Kansas and Missouri, though under a different name. During the war years he called himself John J. Sly, and under that name was wanted for crimes in four states, and by crimes I don't mean barroom brawls and robbery. He and his men laid siege to a pro-Union town called West Athens and finally burned it to the ground, raping the women, killing everyone including children after entering the town under a flag of truce.

"The end of the war found Siringo a wanted man, but oddly a man without a record. He was John J. Sly—whereabouts unknown, antecedents unknown, appearance unknown."

"Where was he?" Ruff asked.

"Still in Kansas," Major Corson said, his lips compressed, eyes bitterly cold, "wearing a Union Army uniform."

"Smart," Ruff said.

"That's the trouble with Siringo—he is smart. Too damned smart. He saw that the wind had shifted, knew he would be hung if caught. He threw away his gray uniform, put on homespuns, and walked into the recruiting office, and under his real name he enlisted. I believe," Corson said dryly, "that Siringo received a fifty-dollar enlistment bonus that day."

"You seem to know a lot about this man."

"Oh, I know a lot about him now. When it's too late. At the time no one knew anything about him. The war was winding down. He was a new recruit, a Kansas farmboy who actually distinguished himself in one Western battle and won a field promotion to staff sergeant. There was also a commendation involved."

Colonel MacEnroe had refrained from making any comments. Now Ruff heard him murmur, "The bloody bastard."

"He remained in the army?" Justice asked.

"Yes, he did. He was a soldier at heart, after all. He couldn't risk staying in Kansas. There is, of course, a regulation which prevents any former Confederate officer from holding a commission in the United States Army, but Siringo, having no record, was given the rank of second lieutenant on his commanding officer's recommendation after a battle with Red Cloud's Sioux warriors along the Upper Missouri River near Loisel's Post."

"That was 1870," Ruff said.

"It was."

"Mr. Justice," the colonel put in, "having spent the years after the war doing whatever it is Mr. Justice does when he is not fighting"—the colonel allowed himself a small smile—"had returned to army service by '70."

"Did you know Siringo?" Major Corson asked.

"No. I just don't recall the man. I was serving with Crook during '70 and '71."

"Looking back," the major went on, "there are suspicious circumstances surrounding the victory Siringo was said to have won, but it's only another point in a long and vicious career which will probably never be cleared up. To return to what we know: Siringo had by this time summoned two former Sangborne guerrillas to him. Both had been captains in the Confederate Army, and of course had to enter the Union Army as private soldiers—which they did without hesitation, knowing that Siringo would find a way to make it worth their while. There are no known portraits of these two men. Jethro Jewell Cavett was thirty-five years old at this time. A bulky, scowling man with a heavy beard. He has a slight limp and a permanent part in his black hair from a bullet which came that near to removing this piece of scum from the earth. He was with Sangborne before Siringo himself joined the guerrillas. It seems that Cavett took him under a fatherly wing and personally taught Siringo the fine art of guerrilla fighting." The major looked up at Justice, his eyes flinty, his lip slightly trembling. "At Freshwater, Missouri, during 1864, Cavett took eighteen women of the town, subjected each to the repeated rape his men were infamous for, then set them afire after pouring coal oil over their naked bodies. They were sent floating down the Missouri River, a sight which is said to have sent Cavett into gales of merry laughter.

"Jethro Jewell Cavett achieved the rank of staff sergeant in the Union Army. He was assigned to the staff of Captain Roscoe Siringo at Laramie garrison."

Ruff Justice rose and walked to the colonel's desk, where he poured himself a drink from the pitcher of water at the colonel's elbow. Resuming his seat, he crossed his long legs at the knee and nodded.

"The third man," Major Corson resumed. "Amos Diggs. He's a real brute, Mr. Justice. As tall as yourself, but twice as wide. Even Siringo apparently couldn't control him. Diggs made sergeant but was busted back. He spent six weeks in the Laramie stockade for attacking another soldier with a sledge hammer. Diggs has no idea what words like 'morality' or 'conscience' might mean. He likes to hurt people, and he's done it plenty of times. Thin red hair, gray eyes, piece of left ear missing."

"All right," Ruff said with a bit of impatience. "I've got that all down mentally. Three men, Siringo, Cavett, and Diggs. I assume they're on the run. Now then, why are they running and why do you want me to find them?"

"Did you ever hear of the Benchmark massacre, Ruff?" Colonel MacEnroe asked his scout.

"I heard of it, yes. I saw it."

"I didn't know that. Then you know what happened. Twenty miners panning gold along Benchmark Creek this side of the Black Hills, out of the holy land the Sioux had staked out, they thought. One morning they were hit by hostiles armed with repeating rifles. All twenty men died, though one, Albert Taylor by name, lingered on for quite a while. He had been scalped, as had the others. Their weapons, mules, and horses had been taken, and according to Taylor as much as thirty thousand dollars in gold dust."

"Which didn't figure for the Sioux, but it was definitely their work," Ruff interjected.

"Partly." MacEnroe leaned back. "This is how it happened, Ruff, and what I would have given to know it at the time! Siringo was riding patrol on the western perimeter when he came upon the Benchmark camp. Investigating, he was shown some of the gold dust the miners were coming up with. Why not? What did they have to fear from the army?

"It stuck in Siringo's mind, and he came up with the idea of arming a band of renegade Sioux under Quincha with new rifles, telling them where they could come by twenty horses and as many mules, promising them that the army would not be in the area on a certain day."

"In exchange for the gold."

"That's it."

"How'd you come to find out about this now?" Ruff asked.

"One of Quincha's men was taken. He was asked where he had gotten the new Winchester he was carrying, and his reply was: 'The soldier gave it to me.' "

"Siringo was already gone."

"Yes, he had resigned his commission the month before, six months after the Benchmark massacre, when Cavett's enlistment had run out and Diggs, who still had a year to go, had been listed as a deserter by the Laramie garrison."

Ruff leaned back, fingertips pressed together. He looked over them at MacEnroe. "Why me, colonel?"

"Because we have nothing on Siringo. After looking into his record deeper we know the kind of man he is, but there was nothing but the testimony of the Sioux warrior—who, by the way, has escaped—and you know what an Indian's word is worth in a court of law. The same goes for using the United States Marshals' organization. There is no legal framework for arresting these three, with the exception of Diggs, who could be brought in for desertion. But, dammit, Ruff, the men are as guilty as sin! Siringo used his position as an army officer to abet the murder of twenty men, and he's gotten away clean."

"Where is he?"

"Colorado."

Ruff smiled. "Can you narrow that down a little, colonel?"

"Denver. Siringo was spotted there by an officer from Fort Vasquez who had served with Siringo at Laramie. He swears it was Siringo, although the man refused to speak to him, refused to recognize him. It puzzled the officer, and he mentioned it to his commanding officer, Lieutenant Colonel Tip Dandridge, who happens to be a friend of mine. Dandridge himself went into Denver with a party of soldiers, but there was no trace of Siringo. It's just as well, probably. Dandridge can be a bit hotheaded; he might have gotten himself into a lot of trouble."

"And you prefer to save the trouble for me," Ruff said with a smile.

"You're used to it," MacEnroe replied, half seriously.

"All right. What do I do?"

"Find the bastards, Ruff. Find them . . . and try to bring them back." His tone of voice indicated he would prefer another solution. Probably there would be no choice. Siringo, not knowing what the army had on him, would fight rather than surrender. "You can draw your pay and turn in your resignation," MacEnroe said. "You can't be under army contract on this job."

"No." Nor could he expect any help from the army if it blew up in his face, Justice knew.

There was a stack of ten double eagles on the colonel's desk, and rising, he said dryly, "Those must be yours, Ruff."

Ruff supposed so too, and he pocketed the gold coins, wondering where the colonel had come by them. Knowing MacEnroe, it was likely the two hundred was out of his own pocket. Major Corson was frowning as if he believed the traveling money was far too much; but MacEnroe knew Ruff's tastes.

Now Justice was in Denver, and through the winter months he had seen no sign of the three wanted men, heard not a whisper. He had begun to believe they were long gone—until the little hired thug with too much whiskey in his belly had come a-hunting.

Justice crossed to his closet and took out his buckskins. He stepped into the fringed trousers and pulled the shirt over his head. The bone-handled skinning knife went into the sheath inside the right boot. The bear-claw necklace went around his throat. The belt holding the big Colt .44 and the razor-sharp bowie was buckled on around his waist. From the closet shelf he took the white, wide-brimmed Stetson hat with the beaded hatband.

The town suit and the ruffled shirt he stuffed into the wicker laundry hamper. He would not need them for a while, perhaps never again.

He was going hunting, and the prey was as savage as anything Justice had ever tracked.

3

The gray horse looked fat and woolly in its winter coat. It pricked its ears with interest as Ruff Justice walked into the Gordon Hostelry on Grand Avenue. The hostler was asleep on a nail keg in the corner, a *Police Gazette* draped over one knee.

Ruff took a curry comb from its nail on the wall and worked over the gray for half an hour. Most of the heavy winter coat was falling out by itself, so he decided against clipping it. The gray, a fifteen-hand mustang with a white mane and tail and a white splotch on its left hindquarter, enjoyed the attention as always, and this time seemed to sense that something was up, that its enforced idleness was nearly at an end.

"Taking him out?" The hostler spoke around a yawn, fisted hands raised in a massive stretch.

"Yes. I'll settle up now."

"Got your saddle?"

"I do."

"I'll check the book then, though you're just about up to date, Mr. Justice."

He was. There was only six dollars owing, and Ruff gave it to him in silver along with two more for a tip. That money might not mean much for a while. Maybe never again. It brightened the hostler's eyes.

"If anybody asks . . ."

"I don't tell 'em nothin', Mr. Justice. Not even last time when they offered me five bucks."

"No?" *Who* had offered five bucks? "When was this, Harvey?"

"Day before yesterday. A big man with red hair came in, asking which was Mr. Justice's horse."

Amos Diggs? Someone was looking around. Ruff doubted the hostler would have kept quiet under the urging of five dollars, but he said nothing. It didn't matter anymore.

Half an hour later Ruff Justice was in the saddle on the gray, moving out into the brilliant sunlight of a Colorado morning. The snow made mirrors of the foothills where it had not yet melted, and the long ranks of pine forest stretched away toward the Rockies.

The gray was pleased to be out and moving. It held its head high and stepped out briskly. The wind was chill off the high mountains, the earth sodden. Here and there new spring grass showed through the melting patches of snow.

Ruff's mission seemed an impossible one, but he did not think it was that. He knew the men were not in Denver; a winter's careful searching had convinced him of that. Yet they were nearby. Someone had contacted Hicks. Someone, possibly Diggs, had been to the stable asking about Ruff.

The land was wide and wild, but very few men were capable of hiding out in it. The reason was simple—to hide out meant being entirely self-sufficient, and Ruff doubted Siringo and his men were competent to winter out living off the land.

Therefore they had to be either holed up in a

town near Denver or drawing supplies from such a town. Despite the breadth of the land it was sparsely populated, and people having little else to do in the dead of winter noted all comings and goings. If Siringo was around he would have been seen—all strangers were treated with a deal of interest and suspicion.

There were only a handful of settlements near Denver, and Ruff meant to ask around each in turn. He felt confident in his ability to find Siringo. It was after he found the man that the trouble would begin.

Long flights of geese winging northward cut Vs across the April skies. Ruff startled a winter-coated masked badger out on the prowl. The fierce little creature turned challengingly and waddled away toward its den.

The stream he followed was fringed with ice. The snow, rapidly melting now, was twelve inches deep. The wind rumbled the long ranks of pines. Above it all the Rockies towered, and somewhere at the base of Mount Evans, a pyramid-shaped mountain which dominated the smaller summits, lay the mining town of Lode, Ruff's first stop.

He camped out that night beneath the clear cold stars listening to the muted hoots of the owls and the wind songs playing in the tall pines, once hearing the distant, mournful howl of a wolf.

He slept with a Colt in his hand, for he had seen them earlier in the day, flitting through the forest. The Utes too had awakened from their winter sleep. The Utes too would be hunting.

Ruff had been among the Utes, but he could not say he understood these mountain people. He had been welcomed by the Moache Utes, hunted by the Wiminuche. They were at once generous and deadly, solemn and superstitious, their heads filled with tales of mountain spirits and sky cougars. Who was to say they were not right? A night spent alone in the high-up mountains peeled back the hide which encases a man's soul, and the old notions, the fears of atavistic man, began to stir again. Ruff himself had seen things for which there was no explanation.

Morning dawned clear. There was a brief orange flush across the snowfields, a rosy hue to the eastern sky, and then the rising sun limned the horizon with pure gold, lighting the tall pines at the tips with brilliant stars.

Justice entered Lode in midafternoon.

Lode was a mining town, pure and simple. Its citizens had no use for a newspaper, schools, churches, or sheriff's office. They saw to their own peacekeeping. It was a town built hurriedly, its only ambition to strip the surrounding hills of precious ore. It sheltered the miners, fed them, amused them. There were thirteen saloons, two whorehouses, one brick bank. The miners needed and wanted nothing else.

The town was a low, dirty, colorless collection of shacks set in a low, dirty, colorless valley. Ruff sat the gray, looking down on Lode, knowing he was looking at a town which would be dead in a matter of years, a place where no one had anything of himself invested, and for that reason alone it was doomed.

Above the town, smelters spewed sulfuric waste into the clear cold air. The slopes of the hills had been stripped for timbers, and the winter rains had gouged deep gullies into the unprotected soil. Mules dragged heavy carts along a crooked, washboarded road. From somewhere in the town a gunshot rang out. Ruff rode on in, expecting little.

He tried the general merchandise store first. It was run by a middle-aged, balding Swede and his burly wife, who would have made two of the storekeeper. Here, if Siringo was in the area, he would come for his provisions.

"No, no," the Swede continued to say as he worked stocking his shelves.

"One of them is a big redheaded man with gray eyes. Part of his left ear is missing."

"No, no. I don't see nobody's ears." The Swede shook his head. "Just a minute, Mrs. Bennett."

"One's a bulky man with black hair, probably wearing a beard."

"I got a hundred customers look just like that. Coming, Mrs. Bennett. Listen, mister, I got work to do."

"This one then?" Ruff asked, holding out the daguerreotype of Roscoe Siringo.

"No. Maybe. No. I don't know."

"He's older now, maybe a little less hair."

"I don't know, mister. You have a badge or something?" he asked.

"No."

"I don't see him. Or the others. I don't know. I look at their money, not at their faces. What do I know? Coming, Mrs. Bennett!"

Ruff was starting to get the evil eye from the Swede's huge wife, and he believed the little man when he said he knew nothing about the three outlaws, so, with an elaborate bow to the Swede's wife, he made his way out into the cold afternoon.

A heavy freight wagon was sloughing up the main street. A woman in red silk was picking her way across the planks which were laid at the corners across the churned-up mud of Lode's thoroughfares. From upcountry the heavy thunking of a stamp mill echoed down the valley.

Ruff stepped into the gray's saddle and walked it across the street to the Gilded Rose Saloon.

Inside it was relatively quiet, the mines still being in operation. A weary, lonely-looking cowhand already past his prime sat nursing a whiskey at the puncheon bar. Two gamblers, looking up anxiously as Ruff entered through the faded green door, returned to their two-handed solitaire as Justice turned toward the bar. A blonde with pouched eyes eyed him from the corner, her faded smile more repulsive than encouraging.

"Coffee?" Ruff asked of the bartender, who wore a brown suit, worn at the elbows, against the chill of the saloon.

"If you'll wait a minute. I smell it boiling in back now."

"Fine." Ruff turned his back on the bar and stared at the occupants of the room. They weren't likely material, but then all they needed was a pair of eyes. He spoke to the cowhand. "Buy you a drink?"

That lifted him out of his seat quickly enough. He sauntered to where Ruff stood, wobbling slightly on his high-heeled boots. "Name's Joe Gant," the stubby cowboy said. Ruff shook his hand and settled into a long conversation. He found out nothing about Siringo, Cavett, and Diggs, but learned more than he ever wanted to know about the Bozeman and Goodnight-Loving trails, about a cowboy's miseries and the character of nature's most stupid and vicious creation, the longhorn steer.

Ruff bought the cowboy another drink and slid down the counter a way to talk to the bartender.

"Seen Roscoe Siringo?" Ruff asked in a low voice.

"Who?" The barkeep continued to dry the glasses.

"Siringo. Probably ain't using that name now." Ruff smiled knowingly. "We used to run together down in Abilene."

"Never heard of him."

"Here's a picture," Justice said, sliding the daguerreotype across the counter. The bartender didn't even look at it.

"Mister, way it is here, with me, is I don't know anybody. Get me?"

"Sure." Ruff winked and pocketed the picture. "Smart way to be. All the same, if you remember anything, I might make it worth your while."

"Where are you staying?"

"Thought I'd sleep out," Ruff said with another wink. "Feel safer out in the open."

Three miners, their faces black and gritty, their legs muddy to the knees, came in, and the bartender went to serve them, throwing Ruff a last measuring glance. Justice drank his coffee and left the saloon, going to the hotel on the corner. There had been no point in telling the bartender where he was going to sleep. This was a strange town, and they likely banded together against outsiders as they do in all small towns. Maybe the man had never heard of or seen Siringo. Then again, perhaps he had.

Ruff signed in under an alias, paid for the night in advance, and took the brass key the room clerk gave him. Going upstairs, he found the room down a narrow, unlighted corridor. Entering, he looked around, noticed he had a window overlooking the main street, and tossed his saddle in the corner.

Ruff put his rifle down on the bed and then tugged the bed to the far wall. He locked the door, then lay down on the bed, crossed boots on the bedrail, hands behind his head. The ceiling was stained, he noticed. The room had a sour smell. He wondered how many nights he would have to spend in rooms no better than this one.

Hunting a man is slow work. Nights creep past, days drag, the trail grows long and dusty. The danger lies in being lulled by the boredom. One day it would happen, he would find Siringo and there would be a sudden, violent response. He had to be ready when it happened.

Justice rose and looked out the grimy window at the street, seeing little. The men's faces were hidden by their hatbrims. Siringo, he knew, would not be working in a mine. He would be working another deadly scheme or drawing one up.

Siringo too would grow bored, however. He would come into this town or one like it to gamble or have a drink, maybe for a woman. And he would be seen.

Ruff put on his hat. There was a tap at the door, and he turned, frowning. He unholstered his Colt and held it in his right hand as he opened the door with his left. There was no need for it.

The tired, blurred-looking blonde from the saloon stood there smiling.

"I saw you come over here. I thought you might want some company."

"Unfortunately, I was just going out," Ruff said gently.

"Too bad." She looked him up and down and shook her head regretfully. "Well, if you change your mind later, you know where to find me."

"I do." Ruff eased her out of the room, waited a minute, and went out himself. From behind one of the hotel-room doors came the sounds of two drunks arguing about a lost whiskey bottle.

Outside, the streets were filling up as the miners headed home. The sun was already almost to the peaks of the mountains to the west. The shadows bled out at the bases of the buildings along the street.

Ruff stood on the corner, watching. On other occasions he had found the best informants to be kids. Kids who saw everything and weren't reluctant to talk about what they saw. Lode seemed to be short on kids—few of the miners had families with them.

He walked the main street, peering into the saloons, watching the sea of dark faces, recognizing no one. At sundown he walked the gray to a nearby stable, stopped to have a filling, greasy meal of beef and potatoes in the hotel dining room, and went up to bed.

It had been some time since Ruff had spent the day in the saddle, and he fell off to sleep, three leering faces spinning through his dreams.

He came suddenly alert sometime after midnight. The silver moon was peering in his window. The streets below were silent.

What had awakened him?

He lay utterly still, even his breathing throttled down to a whisper. He could hear the blood murmuring in his ears.

He heard it then. Outside his door a floorboard squeaked. Ruff's hand snaked out for his Colt, which was slung from the headboard. His fingers hadn't closed around it when the door popped open on broken hinges.

The shotgun roared twice in the darkness, and Ruff grabbed his Colt and rolled to the floor, firing back toward the empty doorway.

Someone was running back down the corridor, but by the time Ruff, moving cautiously so as not to walk into a load of buckshot, reached the hall, he was gone. Other doors along the corridor had burst open and men in nightshirts and longjohns stood gawking at Ruff's door. Gunsmoke still rolled out of his room, and Justice turned back, crossing the room to throw open the window before he lit his lamp.

The floor where the bed had been before Ruff moved it was torn to splinters from a double load of buckshot. Justice felt a chill creep along his spine. He holstered his gun and was pulling his buckskins on when the room clerk, half asleep, face and eyes red, reached the room and stood gaping at the damage.

"I'll want another room," Justice said.

"The door . . . the floor . . ."

"Find the man that just went out of here. What were you doing, sleeping down at the desk?"

"The door. Look at that."

Ruff grunted, flipped his gunbelt around his waist, grabbed his hat, and went out. So far as he knew, only one person had followed him to his room. He was going out to find himself a blonde.

The saloon was still open. A handful of dedicated drinkers were hanging on, speaking in low voices. Ruff strode across the sawdust-littered floor to the barkeeper.

"Where's that girl who works here?"

"Which one?" the bartender asked, his voice surly.

"The blonde."

"I don't know." He turned away, and Ruff yanked him violently back, pulling him halfway across the bar by his coat front.

"Where is she?"

The barkeep looked deep into those ice-blue eyes and nodded. "All right. It's Tillie," he gasped. "She's in the back."

"Show me."

The bartender nodded, and Ruff let him go. Justice followed him to a narrow doorway and through, past dark, sleazy cribs to a door which had once been painted red.

"In there," the bartender said.

"You're going with me," Ruff told him, and the man sighed. He knocked on the door, getting no response.

"Open it."

"There might be someone in there with her," he protested.

"Tough. I don't embarrass easy. Open it."

The man swung the door open and peered cautiously in. "Tillie?" The next sound he made was a strangled curse. He turned around, his face ashen. Ruff thought he was going to be sick.

He shoved the bartender aside and went into the room, where a lamp burned low, casting a yellow glow across the body which lay on the floor.

"Oh, Jesus. Who'd do it to the poor old thing?" the bartender moaned. "Poor old Tillie."

Poor old Tillie was sprawled on the floor, lying in a dark pool of her own blood. Her throat had been slashed viciously. She lay there, eyes staring up at them, her face contorted still by fear and pain.

"Why, why?"

Ruff glanced at the barkeep, who had his face buried in his hands. Justice only wanted to know *who*. He figured he knew why this had been done.

Unless there was some amazing coincidence at work, the death of Tillie was tied in with Ruff himself. She had tailed him to the hotel and located his room. Someone had made a try at killing Ruff. Now Tillie was dead.

"Did you see anybody talking to her earlier?" Ruff asked.

"What?" the man asked from out of the fog of shock. "Everyone talks to Tillie. Everyone knows her."

"She have a special man?"

"She treated them all special, mister. You'da had to know Tillie."

"Where'd she live?"

"Here. She lived here." He looked around the drab room. There were chintz curtains hung on the wall where there was no window. A faded overstuffed chair sat in the corner. A well-used bed was shoved up against the wall.

"You recall any special man—a stranger, maybe—you let me know," Ruff said.

"Sure. Sure."

Ruff turned and walked out of the room, striding across the saloon, with relief breaking out into the cold night air. He stood taking deep breaths, watching the stars shift past behind a thin screen of high clouds.

"You're close, old man," he told himself. "Very close."

Unless he had other enemies, there was but one

explanation for this. For Hicks in Denver, for Tillie, for the man with the shotgun. They knew he was on his trail and Siringo didn't like it a bit.

Nobody had bothered trying to warn Ruff off the trail—maybe they knew it would do no good. He had to be killed or he would find them. He hadn't quit on a job yet, and this wasn't going to be the first.

He walked back to the hotel, paid the clerk to run up and fetch his rifle and saddle, and checked out.

"But your new room is all ready."

"Sorry. I just decided that I don't care much for this place."

Ruff nodded, shouldered his saddle, picked up his Spencer carbine, and walked out onto the street. He moved cautiously toward the stable where the gray was being kept. There was no one in the hay-and-dung-smelling building when he reached it, so Justice climbed the ladder to the loft and made a bed out of hay. Then he lay back, Colt in hand, arms crossed, and, amazingly, slept.

In the morning he startled the sleepy-eyed stablehand who was himself crawling out of a bed of straw.

"You can't sleep up there," he said.

"How much?"

"Dollar'll do it."

Ruff tossed him a dollar, left instructions for graining the gray, and went out into the dawn street of Lode. It was quiet still, although the miners were beginning to rise. Ruff had breakfast in the greasy restaurant before it filled up and was out on the street again a little after six.

He began prowling the streets, talking to the idlers, the gamblers, the transients, the pickpockets, the shadowy people who haunted Lode as they haunted every boom town looking for the main chance.

It was noon before he found the man he wanted. Small, whiskered, wearing a dark suit, chewing an enormous wad of tobacco, he called himself Jim Wyatt.

"Yeah, I heard about it. Terrible thing. Woman hadn't done a damn thing to anyone. Nothing that didn't feel good, anyway. Can't figure why any-one'd kill 'er."

"She always stay at the Gilded Rose, did she?"

"Yes. Most times." The man leaned back against the wall, staying in the narrow ribbon of shade cast by the overhead awning.

"Most times?"

"Well, I recollect she had some kind of special customer out toward Antler Creek."

"No one else said anything about that."

"No? Well, I believe Tilly was supposed to not say anything about it. She wouldn't've told me, but I was ready for her one day and she kind of had to tell me, you see. I was mad enough to brain her . . . sounds terrible to say that now, don't it? Yeah, Antler Creek, and from the way she told me I figured it wasn't the first time. Must've paid her real good to trek all that way in winter, don't you think?"

"I'd say so. Any idea who it was?"

"Maybe some secretive old prospector who thinks he's on to the mother lode and don't want to leave." The man shrugged. "Me, I figured it was an outlaw. Makes sense, don't it?"

It did to Ruff Justice. An hour later he was saddled, and after inquiring of the stablehand, he was riding north by west, heading higher into the foothills, angling toward Antler Creek, which was said to lie beyond the hills.

Toward Antler Creek and a secretive man who had known Tillie very well.

4

He rode into the high country where the cold winds blew. The spruce forests were broken by patches of white aspen, just now beginning to bud. The Rockies towered above him, and the steely Antler Creek slid past down rocky chutes, winding its way seaward. Ruff Justice kept to the forest, the gray walking silently over the litter of pine needles, snowmelt, layered humus.

He paused on the narrow rocky outcropping and looked out across the pristine valley below. There had to be a cabin, a lean-to, a dugout somewhere. Unless the mysterious man had already fled, he would be there.

The gray tossed its head and blew, and Ruff patted its neck. He glanced toward the skies. The weather would hold for a few days at least. He had no wish to be caught out in a spring storm.

Ruff tugged his hat down, shifted his Spencer rifle to his right hand, and clicked the horse into motion.

Entering the forest again, he walked the gray upland, eyes still searching. When he came upon it it wasn't his eyes which made the discovery.

He smelled smoke and immediately reined in.

It was definitely smoke and from the north, along the Antler. He moved down into a narrow valley where a pencil-thin stream sang past, winding its way toward the Antler below.

Coming out of the trees, he saw it. Not fifty yards away was a small tumble-down cabin, its roof steeply pitched against winter snows. Made of poles and sod, it had been thrown up hastily with the materials at hand, but seemed well made for all of that.

Gray smoke rose in heavy wreaths from the stone chimney. Ruff circled back into the forest, walking the gray in a half circle through the damp, dark pines.

He spotted a mule behind the house, a pile of gear thrown on the ground beside it. The mule's head came around, smelling Ruff's horse.

Justice decided to take the chance and go straight in. He was not far from the back of the house. No one inside would be able to see him approach from the back. Cocking his rifle, he heeled the gray, lifting it into a canter.

He held his breath crossing the open space between forest and cabin, but no cry was raised, no shots rang out. Ruff dismounted on the run and dashed for the back of the house, leaning his back against it as his eyes searched the yard, the woods beyond.

The gray, reins dangling free, had begun to nibble at the grass before Ruff, rifle in front of him, began working his way toward the front of the house.

The front door stood open a crack, and from within Justice heard the sounds of low humming. He was to the door in three strides, and he booted

it open, lunging sideways through the opening, his
rifle coming level.

"Howdy. You're late for dinner. Have a sit-
down. There's a jug on the mantel."

Ruff lowered his rifle. The old man facing him
wore a long white beard and a buffalo coat which
reached to his ankles. His cheek was distended by
a huge chaw of tobacco. His nose was bulbous and
red, his eyes blue and twinkling.

" 'Spect you're lookin' for Galloway," he said as
Ruff took a chair behind the wobbly table, plac-
ing his Spencer across it casually so that the
muzzle was still trained on the old man.

"Who's Galloway?"

"Don't know. Don't know where he is—wish to
hell I did. Look at this damned mess!"

Ruff glanced around him. Newspapers and
empty cans littered the floor. The cabin stank of
perspiration and dirt. One chair was broken. The
wall to Ruff's right had been chipped away, apparently by someone's endless knife-throwing prac-
tice.

"You don't have to keep that rifle on me, mister. I'm harmless as a mayfly." He opened his coat
to reveal how harmless he was. He wore no visible
gun. Ruff kept his rifle pointed that way. The
man was not one of the three he hunted, but he
had no way of knowing whether or not he was as-
sociated with them. These old trappers—and that
was what Ruff measured him for—were far more
dangerous than these town slicks with a low-slung
Colt. Half the time those would-be tough boys
couldn't hit their own nose with a pistol.

A man who made his living in rough country,
who lived by his wits, stayed alive because of his

gun, was apt to be a whole lot slower, but he would hit what he aimed at.

"Guess we need a formal introduction," the old man said. "I'm Charlie Dare. Some people have heard of me. I'm a trapper and a trader, and I've been at it a hell of a long time. Since before I had a beard on my face. This is my place."

"Been wintered up here?"

"Hell, no! Think I'd leave a place like this?" He waved an angry arm around the trash-strewn room. "No, sir. I was going over to Salt Lake and this here man said he'd give me fifty real dollars if I'd let him winter here. I didn't like him, but I liked the shine of his money. I let him stay on, and away I walked. Just got back, and this is what I found. He's gone—lucky thing or I'd crack Galloway's head for him. Man's the only thing that'll foul up his own nest. Live in his own trash heap. Me, it makes me sick. One reason I left that civilization of yours all them years ago."

"What did this Galloway look like?" Ruff wanted to know. He had noticed the pound can of beans on the table. Half eaten, it was only now beginning to develop mold. Galloway hadn't been gone long. The timing fit.

"Tall man, taller'n you. Red hair." The old man shrugged. "Can't tell you about eyes or birthmarks," he added dryly. "Had a piece of one ear shot off."

Diggs.

"He didn't appear quite right to me," Charlie Dare went on. "In the head, I mean. Got a funny look in his eyes from time to time. But like I say, I was leaving, he had fifty bucks . . . only wish he wasn't such a damned pig. I got to clean this place up, get rid of the cans, them newspapers. Already took a wagonload of whiskey bottles out and buried them. That and a pink lady's petticoat." He winked. "I guess his winter wasn't all that lonely."

"Maybe he wore it," Ruff said.

He hadn't. He had gotten it from Tillie—maybe a last remembrance before he hired her to do his dirty work and then killed her to sever the link between them.

"You don't know where he went?" Ruff asked.

"Didn't say," Dare said. He had begun stuffing a burlap sack full of trash. "Say, you going to shoot me or help me out?"

Ruff grinned. "I'll help," he said.

Together they cleaned the place up, taking the trash to a gully Dare showed him. There they caved the bank in over the trash. Returning to the shack, Dare commented: "He did say something about wanting to stay here until spring. Then he was going to make a killing in the silver business, he said. I told him all the silver claims around here were old ones, tapped out or owned by the big companies, but that didn't bother Galloway none. Said he knew a little something about silver that I didn't. I didn't press him on it. What's the point? Everyone thinks he's got the mother lode, no one wants to talk about their strikes."

They went into the cabin, and Dare, producing an old granite pot and a sack of coffee, began boiling some up.

"So you don't even know which way Galloway was heading?"

"Mister, I told you all I know," Dare said. "I think he was just trying to impress me anyway. Every other man you meet out here knows where a big strike is to be found. Tell you one thing, if he was talking silver, he don't mean on this side of the mountain—it's been combed over years ago. And if he's talking the western slopes he ain't got long to live anyway."

"Why's that?"

"Why? Utes are in an uproar over there, mister. Two tribes going at it tooth and claw, and any white man gets in the way is going to find himself hairless."

"What are they warring about?" Ruff asked, accepting a cup of steaming coffee from Dare.

"Who the hell knows? They got their ways. War is their life—they're brought up on fighting, it's their way."

"But a full-scale war usually has a reason."

"Yeah, but that don't mean a white man would understand them any more than they'd understand why we go off to war for some of the piddlin' reasons we use. Maybe someone took off with the chief's third wife or spit on someone's ancestor's bones. All I know is I'm goin' clear around on my way out, and if you've got any sense, you'll go the same way."

"Who said I was going to the western slopes?"

"Mister, you got that look in your eyes. You're going. Wherever Galloway went, you'll be behind him. I don't expect I can talk you out of it, I'm just tellin' you what it's like over there right now."

They spent the night in the cabin and rode out the following morning while the dawn lit up the pines, which were hung with ice, setting them to sparkling like jewels. Steam issued from the nostrils of the gray and from Charlie Dare's flop-eared mule. The snow crackled underfoot. Antler Creek gurgled past.

"Hate to be leavin'," Charlie Dare said.

"Why are you?"

"Pelts are played out. Too many folks movin' in. Greeners that don't know a beaver from a bobcat, lookin' for something, I don't know what, maybe expectin' to find gold nuggets on the ground, silver veins a mile wide. Colorado's gettin' as bad as California. A hundred men took ninety percent of the gold in California, twenty thousand latecomers divided the other ten. Gamblers and alley artists took most of that back. It's happenin' here. City folks, not knowin what they need to survive out here. Well—I can't give lessons. They'll come; my kind's got to move along. At least some poor bastard'll have a cabin next winter."

They rode higher into the hills, and the wind began to grow cold. Ruff took his own buffalo coat from his roll and bundled up in it.

"Up ahead is Frenchman's Pass," Charlie said, lifting a gnarled finger. "That was named for LaFortune. Hell of a good trapper, maybe four and a half feet tall he was. Grizzly took his head off one spring. That's the straightest way west, but it ain't the way I'm goin'. I'll be riding the ridges, the backbone of this country, north. Steerin' clear of Utes. Want to keep this sparse hair of mine. You, if you're bound and determined, will have to take Frenchman's."

They camped that night in a little teacup valley where high-rising, slate-gray cliffs shielded them from the howling wind.

They let the fire burn to golden embers as they finished their last cup of coffee. Dare spun out yarns of the old days, the days when there were but a handful of white men in these mountains, each living in fear of his life every moment.

"But they were men," Dare said. "Hair and horns on some of 'em. Tough as leather. So tough the beasts wouldn't kill 'em, knowin' they couldn't chew 'em. The Indians in them days had no weapons but their bows and arrows. They was frightened of the thunder a rifle spewed out. It took a while for them to discover that our rifles only fired once.

"Them days a man would give you all his wives, all his horses, a hundred dollars in furs for one beat-up rifle-musket. Didn't dare make a trade like that. The bow and arrow was a better weapon for 'em, but havin' a rifle seemed to make 'em bold. Once they had one they just had to make a war. We'd kill a man who'd given an Indian a rifle—had to. Self-preservation."

Dare's narrative was broken by a savage wind-borne sound. A deep and mournful howl, but unlike the howl of a wolf, which it resembled, it seemed to carry threat, a rising, ululating cry which drifted with the wind, which echoed down the long canyons and sent a creeping chill up a man's spine. It was a voice from a frozen hell, a challenge to man's smallness, savage nature rising up to voice an ominous war cry.

"What in the hell is that?" Ruff asked. He reached for his rifle automatically, although the sound seemed to come from a great distance.

"That, my friend," Charlie Dare said, "is the Windwolf."

"The what?"

"Windwolf, friend. Oh, it's nothing but the way the wind howls down through these canyons at night, but to the Utes it's somethin' else. There's a legend about the Windwolf."

"There usually is."

"Yes." Dare leaned back against his saddle and lit his stubby pipe. "This one, if you've been out here alone long enough, well, a man might start to believe it. A man who's seen enough."

"How's it go?"

"Windwolf legend? Well, it seems that once there was a medicine man belonging to one or another of these small Ute tribes. He loved a woman named Dawn Fire. One night the neighboring Utes came into the camp and there was a fierce battle. Dawn Fire was killed and the medicine man, trying to save her, was mortal wounded.

"He took a dying vow, he did. He swore he'd come back as a big white wolf. When the wind blew they would be sure to hear him howling over his lost love. And whenever anyone threatened the tribe again Windwolf would be there to help them.

"He might come as a wolf or might come as a man, maybe some other creature, like a white bear, but he would be there and the tribal enemies would be destroyed. Well, that howl you hear is the promise of the Windwolf. And I suppose it's fittin', seein' that the Utes are warring again."

Dare's pipe had gone out, and so had the coals. Ruff rolled up in his bed, staring at the cold stars, thinking of Amos Diggs and Siringo. And for a long time he listened to the wind howling down the canyons, thinking of the great Windwolf which prowled these mountains.

5

They rode higher into the snow-streaked, vast mountain range. Ahead, Frenchman's Pass loomed, showing only as a dark notch between two upthrust peaks. The trail the two men followed was rough and broken, littered with fallen rock and mudslides. At times they tilted perilously out over a drop of five thousand feet and more. Nowhere was there a sign of any other life.

"Up ahead a mile or so," Dare shouted above the wind roar, "I'll be forking off to the north. Take my advice and come along, Justice. This lead you're following is damn slim anyway."

Slim wasn't the word for it. All he had to go on was the fact that Diggs, masquerading as Galloway, had holed up in Dare's shack over the winter. Now he was gone, having bragged to Dare that he was going to make a fortune in silver. Dare's assurance that all of the silver strikes on the eastern slope were played out was sending Ruff to the western slopes. It could be he was following a windwolf of his own, but Ruff hadn't expected this to be quick or easy. He was settled in for the long hunt.

By noon they could see the peaks beyond the

timberline, harsh, barren reaches where the wind gusted the snow, whipping it from the gray rock peaks like long horses' tails. The snap and whip of the keening wind was constant now. The pines were all flagged, the branches able to grow only on the side away from the constant wind. Cedars and spruce grew contorted, twisted and stunted by the constant assault of winter and wind.

Charlie Dare drew up. "It's that way I'm heading, Justice." Ruff, looking north, could see a bootlace of a trail winding along the mountain flanks. "If you've any sense, you'll follow along. The way you're heading, man, that's trouble. You've a pretty scalplock on you, and those Utes will lift it if you give them the chance."

"Thanks for the warning, Charlie. I expect I'll be going on."

"I figured you would. Keep hold of your hair, keep that powder dry."

Dare shook his head, smiled faintly, and then started off down the trail, his lop-eared mule unfailingly following the narrow, treacherous trail. Dare's voice was lifted in a song concerning an Arkansas traveler, and Ruff listened until the man was out of earshot and out of sight.

"It's you and me," Ruff said to the gray, which almost seemed to understand and resent the idea. "You're just missing that old mule," Justice said. "Come along. We've some hard traveling to do."

It was all of that. The trail turned up sharply and Ruff was guiding the gray over shale and rubble half the time, moving up a trail which began to be iced over. The rising peaks on either side shadowed the ledge, and there was deep snow intermittently where spring had never reached.

Darkness settled in quickly, and Justice, glancing down at the drop-off, which was sheer and deadly, decided to make camp early. He had no intention of trying to ride that trail after dark.

He kept his eyes open. The trail where he rode now was barely wide enough for him to avoid dragging his leg against the rising cliff face on his right. Below was a massive gorge where entire forests had slid off to lie dead and bleached, stacked and jumbled like jackstraws.

The wind was a constant howling wash through Frenchman's Pass, and the temperature seemed to drop ten degrees for every thousand feet Ruff made.

He saw the small hollow to the side of the trail just as settling dusk made further travel impossible and he was anticipating the gloomy prospect of spending the night on that narrow ledge.

It opened up on his right, a hollow with a narrow overhang some thirty feet deep. There he would be sheltered from the freezing wind. He turned the gray into the hollow and unsaddled as the last purple light of twilight streaked the mammoth skies above the Rocky Mountain landscape.

He found a jumble of wood blown down from the mountain looming overhead. And he found the cold ashes of another fire.

Ruff Justice smiled. He bent to the ashes. They were cold and damp, but they proved one thing. Someone had passed this way since the last snowfall. Someone crossing to the western slopes where the silver mines prospered, where the Utes were waging their war.

It had to be Amos Diggs. And where Diggs was, there too would be Roscoe Siringo.

Ruff settled in for the night. After seeing to the horse he dined on jerky and hard biscuits washed down with water. He watched the stars explode against the sky, incredibly large and silver, beaming down through time and space. Later the moon rose, spreading a silver sheen across the naked land.

One thing puzzled him.

He had spent much time in Denver in recent months, yet he had heard nothing of a new rich silver strike in this part of the country. Of course it could be that those in the know were keeping close-mouthed about it, but that was unusual for the big men. They had no intention of sneaking out and mining it alone; they were the businessmen, the speculators who went at things in a big way. Half a dozen times Ruff had heard the mine owners proposing new projects, offering to let investors in. For what was needed in this country now was not grit, the determination to go out and stake a claim and work it in secret, but capital.

To make the newer claims profitable mills were needed, smelters, labor, wagons, mules—and none of this was come by secretly. Investors flocked around the owner of a promising claim.

Except this one. Ruff had heard not a whisper, not a rumor of silver this far north, this high up.

How then does a man like Amos Diggs, a brute moron, come to know of it? Through Siringo, of course, but then the question repeats itself. How does Siringo manage to find a claim the shrewdest businessmen in Colorado have overlooked?

It was all possible. It was also unlikely.

Ruff rolled up in his blankets, falling asleep as the cold winds blew, as the strange and haunting growl of the wind in the canyons continued, the voice of the Windwolf, which would be returning to help his troubled people.

Ruff was shivering as he rolled out in the predawn. The temperature had plummeted during the night. With frozen fingers he managed to get a fire started and set his morning coffee to boiling.

The horse eyed him mournfully. Its back was coated with ice, and Ruff had to take a piece of sacking and rub the animal down before he saddled up. By then the coffee was boiling and he settled down over a dark, bitter cup.

An hour later, after checking his weapons, Ruff Justice rode out into the splendor of a new Rocky Mountain morning. It was a sight he had once grown familiar with, and now it greeted him with warm magnificence.

The snowfields were stained rose and orange with the dawn colors on this morning. The purple mountains stood erect and stolid, proud and remorseless against the sky. Deep green velvet stands of timber flowed across the flanks of the mountains and into the rolling hills.

A lone golden eagle soared high against a perfect morning sky.

There was no other man in this world, no soul but that of Ruff Justice, and he threw back his head and laughed out loud, a madman loose on the face of this primitive earth.

He sobered as he rode higher into Frenchman's Pass. On the far side of that weathered notch were three men who wanted him dead. Somewhere above or behind him, to the north or south, were two warring Ute tribes who would be all too happy to tie his scalp to their lances.

"Fun's over," he told the horse, which twitched its ears and plodded on into the teeth of the cold wind. The wind, constant and whining, rose to a gusting shriek as he neared the pass itself. Cold shadows from the towering peaks beside him lay around Ruff Justice.

The horse was laboring as he crested the trail and caught his breath. The view to the west was even more spectacular. Mile upon mile of great mountains twisting together, jutting skyward, running away in convoluted files toward Canada on his right, toward a distant Mexico to his left.

Beyond the mountains lay great high deserts, seen here and there as bald, misty patches between the mountain peaks. Virgin stands of timber stretched out endlessly. It was a hard and glorious country, and Ruff nodded his head once with satisfaction, with the joy of it, before he kneed the gray and started down the long slopes toward the guns of his enemies.

The clouds began to build ominously in late evening, and Ruff glanced skyward frequently, his eyes narrowing. He had seen mountain storms before and had no liking for them.

Lightning would arc from peak to peak, the wind would turn into walls of resistance, and the rain would fall like iron pellets. Trails would wash away, flash floods would engorge the lowlands. Trees would fall and great boulders would be undercut to slide and roll down dangerously.

Ruff was into timber again now, the wind singing in the pines. Snow was light here, travel easy. He found the Ute a mile on.

Lying unmoving in the snow, he was nearly hidden from view, but Ruff managed to pick him out of the background before he rode over him.

He stepped down and had a look. Stone cold dead and stiff, he had been shot in the chest and arm. He had tried to bind up the arm with a piece of cloth, but they had apparently caught up with him. His scalp was peeled back. He was wearing war paint now faded, smeared.

"Fortunes of war," Ruff muttered. One day it would be him and he knew it, but not this time. Somewhere on this day there was a family looking to the mountains waiting for a son or father or husband who would not return.

He was in a battle zone now, and Ruff moved even more cautiously as he returned to the saddle. Shortly before sunset it began to rain.

Great blustering thunder shook the mountains as forked lightning played across the sky. Through the sheer lower clouds Ruff could see the rose-colored sunset. But the higher stacked thunder-heads were opaque, purple-gray, and the rain fell.

There were only scattered, huge drops for the first few minutes, but then the storm settled in and the rain advanced across the forested wilderness in heavy veils. Ruff tugged his hat lower and hunched his shoulders.

He was looking now for a place to camp, knowing that any camp he chose would not be safe in this area. Not with the Utes at war.

He could barely see the horse's head as the twisting rain washed over him. He was already soaked to the bone, shivering with the cold.

"Makes a man wonder about this line of work," he grumbled. He could still be at the Imperial, sitting before the fireplace in the gilt-embellished lobby, speaking to the ladies as the storm raged outside. He saw what he wanted through a gap in the rain.

A great knobby boulder pushed out from the side of a low, pine-clad hill. The rock had been split by the roots of a gigantic blue spruce and the pine still grew there—it or one of its descendants. The sides of the boulder, three horses high, formed an effective windbreak, the overhanging tree formed a crude roof.

Ruff walked the gray through the darkness of the day to the cleft boulder, led it into the gap, and after a quick check for likely rattler hideaways, he unsaddled and sat down on the cold earth, listening to the wind whistle past, the rain drum down, streaming freely through his meager shelter as he slowly, morosely opened a can of tinned beef with his bowie.

His meal was salty, fatty, tasteless. His canteen water washed away the salt, but left the taste of machine-made food in his throat. Ruff drew his blanket up to his neck and settled in to wait out the night and the storm.

The night ended first. Ruff peered upward, saw the gray light of dawn, and rose stiffly. The storm still crackled around him. The floor of his refuge was sodden.

Grumbling, he saddled up and went out into the storm.

He rode downslope, dipping into a small, rainswollen stream, then mounting the far side, where brush, mostly scrub oak, grew in a tangle.

Then he was into the pines again. The sky had lowered still farther, the day growing dark as if the sun had risen briefly, surveyed the miserable day, and immediately sunk again. The pines closed around him; the rain swirled past.

He was into the camp before he had seen it.

Three men leaped to their feet. Two Indians, one white man, and as Ruff reflexively brought his rifle around, the white man cut loose with a hasty shot from his Colt.

Ruff fired back, kicked the gray in the flanks, and leaped the fire, scattering camp equipment and men. He crouched low, twisted, and fired again. By a flash of brilliant lightning Justice saw the face of the white man and knew that he had found Amos Diggs.

Red hair fell into Diggs's face. Hatless he stood, eyes wild and bulging, triggering off three more wild shots which thudded into the timber around Ruff as he raced the gray into the pines.

Ruff dropped from the horse's back, throwing his buffalo coat aside, unholstering his own Colt. He heard one sharp word of command.

"Kill!"

The Indians would be into the woods now. This was their sort of fight, and they would be silent and deadly. Ruff scooped a depression out of the deep pine needles underfoot, lay on his belly, and covered himself.

Then, silent himself, shielded by the darkness of the day, the swirl of rain, he waited. The minutes passed slowly. He heard nothing. He came suddenly alert. A shifting shadowy figure moved through the pines, and Ruff's finger slowly tightened on the trigger of his cocked .44.

The Indian moved from tree to tree, eyes searching, his moccasins silent as he crossed the pine-needle carpet beneath the trees. A burst of lightning illuminated his hawklike features momentarily and caused the warrior to flinch.

He advanced cautiously through the steely mesh of the cold rain. Then he seemed to sense rather than see Ruff and turned toward him, his eyes growing wider yet as he lifted his rifle to his shoulder.

Ruff fired from his prone position, the roar of

the .44 like muffled thunder. The Indian was blown back, the base of his throat torn open by the lead slug. His arms were outflung and he landed on his back, twitching. Ruff never saw him hit.

The tall man leaped to his feet and ran quickly eastward, circling back slowly. He paused behind a mammoth pocked pine trunk and watched the still body of the Indian.

In another moment he saw the second warrior flitting from tree to tree, rifle at the ready. He suddenly saw his companion's body and drew back behind a tree. Ruff could see only the muzzle of his rifle, the tip of a moccasin.

He held his own breath, pulling back behind the tree. Thunder roared across the skies and the earth shook. The trees around him swayed and creaked, rubbing bough against bough as the wind throttled them.

The Indian had moved.

He was no longer behind the tree, and Ruff cursed under his breath, wondering if he had given himself away. Ruff backed away and circled north again. *Where was Diggs?*

The impact of a near bullet tore a fist-sized chunk of white wood from the pine near Ruff's head. Justice went to one knee and fired from the hip with his Colt.

The Indian was nearly on top of him when he cut loose. Whether he was out of ammunition, reverting to some older style of fighting, or battle-crazed, Ruff was never to know, but the Indian, wielding his rifle like a club, charged at Ruff, his mouth open in a scream which could not be heard above the rage and howl of the storm. He meant to crush Ruff's skull, and crush it he would have but for the .44 bullet which tore into his belly.

The Indian crumpled up, writhing in pain. Ruff stepped to him and cut his throat with the bowie.

Moving swiftly, Ruff returned through the trees to the camp where he had seen Diggs. Lightning flashed again, this time striking the treetops. The air was heavy with the scent of sulfur as the rain washed down.

Justice wiped his long hair out of his eyes and crept on cat feet toward the clearing.

Gone.

Diggs had run. It took no expert tracker to read the sign. Ruff found where Diggs had mounted his horse, found the deeply carved tracks of the horse itself. He had sent the Utes out to do their work and then had fled.

Or that was what the sign indicated. Ruff wasn't green enough to not be alert to the possibility that Diggs had circled back himself. As he moved now, he retained his caution. The gray he found rain-streaked, miserable, staring at him accusingly beneath the pines. It took a bit more searching to find his rifle, but Justice eventually did.

Then he mounted, returned to the camp, and started trailing the big man. Before long the rain would wash out his tracks, but Justice would at least know his general direction—if Diggs wasn't laying a false trail.

That would be about all Justice did know. He did not know, for example, where Diggs was heading, what he was doing in the mountains with two Indians, where Siringo might be, what the business of a silver strike was about. Small things like that.

He knew one thing. Diggs couldn't run that far or that fast. Nor could Jethro Cavett and Siringo. They had the hunter on their trail, and sooner or later they would have to stand up and make their fight. Ruff would leave them no choice, no choice at all.

6

The rain thundered down, and Diggs's tracks were soon lost to the elements. Ruff Justice, sitting the woebegone gray on a wooded knoll, looked down the long valley. The earth fell away at the horse's feet. There was nothing to be seen but rank after rank of timber.

There were no towns on this side of the mountains, Ruff knew, but there had to be something. Diggs had come this way—unless Ruff had badly underestimated the redheaded man—and if there was a silver strike in the vicinity there must be some indication of it. They would have to clear timber to use in shoring up the mine shafts. The miners would need some sort of shelter, even if it was only tents. There would have to be a road for the ore to be carted along; unless they had their own mill, they would have to haul to Denver, and Ruff saw no sign of an ore mill. Nor of a road.

Perhaps the whole thing was a smokescreen thrown up by Diggs to cover the real aim of Siringo and his gang. Looking from this side of the mountain, Ruff was inclined to believe that was the case.

Nothing disturbed the primitive wilderness.

There was no smoke rising to meet the dark clouds, no sign of man-made structures. No sign that anything on two legs had ever crossed this broad and savage land.

Ruff glanced upward again. The skies were even darker. The day grew cold and the snow began to fall.

He moved slowly through the woods, cloaked in a mantle of swirling snow. The scream when it came echoed down the mountainside. It rang pathetically in the air, was picked up and tossed by the wind, and then faded away. Frowning, Justice turned his horse southward, slipping his rifle from its protective buckskin sheath.

Diggs? He had no idea. More likely it was the Utes having at each other, but he had to know. Maybe, he thought with grim amusement, the Indians have got Siringo, Diggs, and Cavett. There would be a kind of justice in that. They who had used the Indians to do their own murders being scalped and skinned by the Utes.

That wasn't at all what it was, though. The scream rose again, so near that Justice jerked his head around, peering with narrowed probing eyes into the sheets of snow surrounding him.

He saw her then.

A woman on the ground, and around her three warriors. A gathering basket was where it had fallen, its contents spread across the ground. The bucks were about to have at her. Her buckskin dress had been ripped from her and thrown to one side.

She screamed again, and Ruff Justice fired.

The man was trying to mount the fighting woman when Ruff's .56 Spencer spoke and he was blasted from her, turning a somersault, his blood spraying the new snow. The other two spun toward Ruff, snatching for their weapons.

The big .56 spoke again and the bullet punched through the second man's belly, shattering his spine as it exited, killing him instantly. Shifting his sights, Ruff touched off again, his muzzle exploding with flame even as the Indian, Winchester to his shoulder, fired. Ruff heard the whip of a bullet past his head and flinched involuntarily. The Indian never flinched. The bullet from the Spencer thumped into the Indian's chest, spinning him around, and he lay still, arms outflung, the life leaking out of his body.

Ruff swung a leg over the gray's neck and slipped to the earth, walking forward through the snow, his eyes alert and active. The woman sat watching him with great brown eyes, naked against the snow, her teeth chattering.

She was young and cold and quite beautiful, with full high breasts, slim waist, flaring hips, tapered thighs firm with the muscle tone of one who does much walking.

"Get dressed," he told her, looking over his enemies to make sure they were not only down but out. She simply stared as the snow swirled around them. "Get dressed. You'll freeze to death!"

He searched his memory for the Ute words. He had once wintered up with a Ute girl named Yarna, but he hadn't had much occasion to learn how to say "Get dressed"—it had mostly been the reverse. Too, there were many dialects among the various mountain tribes.

"Get dressed," he repeated in the Ute tongue he knew.

"You!" Her voice was a breathless gasp, and Ruff frowned. He did not know this woman, had never seen her. The shifting snow drifted between them, the long winds blew. The girl picked up her dress and covered herself. Still she stood staring at Justice until he nodded, smiled, and started away, leading his gray horse.

He looked back once through the snow and thought he saw her, still standing, still watching, but it might have been illusion in this light, under these conditions.

He shook aside thoughts of the lovely Indian girl and, mounting his gray, headed off downslope again. He had gone half a mile when it happened. Some trick of the wind, some confusion of the senses, some suggestibility made the impossible occur.

Ruff saw the movement beside the trail, and he reined up quickly, silently drawing his rifle free again. He saw immediately that it was not a man, but what it was he did not know. A shadow, an illusion sketched by the falling snow. It was very large, quick and furtive. It was there and then it was not. Before Ruff could react it was gone—but for just a moment it had seemed to be a wolf, a wolf larger than any he had ever seen.

He had nearly pushed the image from his mind when the cry came again. Long, mournful, vengeful, and proud. The Windwolf howling against the storm.

Ruff Justice was hardly a superstitious man, but just then, under those circumstances, the storm confusing the senses, he could almost believe that he had seen it, that even now it stalked the mountains, searching the enemies of its people.

A man alone in these mountains saw much; it was best not to believe half of it. Ruff kneed the gray and rode forward down the mountain slope.

* * *

It came suddenly into view shortly before night-fall.

A collection of shacks and tents frosted by the new snow, set on a bench above a nameless creek. Justice halted his horse and stepped down, study-ing the white settlement. Slowly he smiled. This was it.

The silver town. It had to be. The wood of the shacks was all new and green, unweathered. The town itself—it was a courtesy to call it a town—had existed only for a matter of weeks, months at the most. The wind drifted Ruff's hair across his face. His cold blue eyes searched the surrounding hills, looking for signs of mining activity. Eventually he spotted it. High on the mountain slope across the creek a shaft mouth yawned. No one was working it today. The men would be huddled together, trying to keep warm, drinking whiskey, playing cards.

And perhaps among them were Siringo and his gang.

It had to be, he thought. Could there be an-other new mining camp in this country? How, he wondered idly, were these men protecting them-selves from the rampaging Utes? He saw no guards posted, no sign of activity out of doors. The place might have been deserted except for the wisps of gray smoke which rose from the black iron stovepipes, twisting skyward to merge with the grayness of the lowering skies.

Ruff Justice rode in.

The snow was melting on the ground, the storm losing its power, but massive dark clouds clotted the tiny valley. Great black webs had been spun from peak to peak. The wind was unabated.

Justice reined up beside a two-story building,

the only one in the ramshackle town. Stepping down onto the muddy ground, he stripped off his buffalo coat, checked the loads in his Colt, shifted his bowie, and stood looking around him.

No one was in the streets. Odd, if they knew the Utes were warring, not to have some sort of home guard. Maybe they didn't know. He walked slowly to the main street—if it could be called that. It was gouged mud, dark and slick with water. He could now hear the sounds of voices raised in argument from the two-story building. The town wasn't completely deserted.

Ruff slowly let his eyes search the town. A smith's shop, a general store set up in an old army tent, the saloon before which he now stood, and beyond the stable across the street dozens of tents and shacks thrown up by the miners.

He looked again at the saloon, then turned away, searching for a back door. If Siringo was in there he didn't want to walk in the front way.

There was a back door, but it was locked. With a little encouragement from the bowie the barrel lock slid free, however, and Justice stepped into a dark storeroom. He left the door unlocked behind him.

The storeroom smelled of sawdust and vinegar. Ruff stretched out a hand and felt the barrels which would be whiskey, the only antidote for cold and boredom in this part of the country.

Ahead he saw a ribbon of light at floor level, and from beyond that voices drifted. Ruff went to the door, opened it a crack, and stood watching. He could see a bar which was nothing more than a long plank laid over two barrels. An open crate of whiskey bottles was tilted against the wall behind the bar. A whiskey barrel sat to one side.

The wall in back of the bar was decorated with pictures of ladies in their corsets cut out of some catalogue or magazine. Smoke hung heavy in the air, both woodsmoke and tobacco smoke.

He could see no one but the bartender, who was as burly as that trade requires a man to be, thick and dark and scowling, with a turned-down mustache and a bent nose.

Ruff pushed on in through the door. The bartender's head came around, his scowl deepening.

"Hey, what the hell are you doing in there!"

Ruff's eyes were sweeping the room, his hand near the butt of his holstered Colt. There were two dozen men in the saloon. They might have been the same men as he had seen in Lode in the Gilded Rose. They had the same dark faces, the same work-toughened hands, the same weary eyes, the same good-natured mouths. He did not see Siringo, or Diggs, or Cavett.

"Did you hear me, mister? What the hell were you doing in my storeroom?"

"Sorry," Ruff said mildly. "The door was open and I came in. I didn't know I wasn't supposed to use that entrance."

"Door was open? Damn that Murphy, I've told him a hundred times about leaving that door open." The bartender got back to work, still muttering. Murphy, whoever he was, would catch hell in the morning.

Ruff walked over to the bar, waited until a miner was served, and asked for coffee.

"Coffee? Suppose I've got some," the bartender said, frowning. "My own stuff. Cost you a dollar. I can't get along pouring out coffee, you know."

Ruff waved a hand. "It's all right. Whatever you say." He stood negligently against the wall beside the bar. His eyes were anything but casual as they again searched the room, studying each face, trying to see behind the beards, behind the eyes.

Diggs he had seen and would not forget. Siringo, unless he had changed a lot, Ruff would recognize. Cavett was a mystery. Bulky, scowling, black-haired, with a bullet part along his scalp from a near miss. A man who had set women afire and laughed as they burned. Scratch that. Not a *man*. A man gets no pleasure out of a thing like that. Cavett was an animal, filth. Another of these moronic savages that a primitive tribe would have stoned to death. And rightly so.

"What the hell are you looking at?"

Whatever Ruff had been looking at, it was not the nearly bald, muscular man in the red-checked shirt who sat drunkenly staring at Justice from across his whiskey-barrel table.

"Nothing," Justice said mildly. "Forget it, friend."

The bartender had returned with his coffee, and Ruff slid a dollar across the plank.

"Whadya mean, nothin'!" the voice behind Ruff roared. "Whadya mean turnin' your back on me?"

Ruff sighed slowly. Couldn't these men find some other way to amuse themselves? Someone snorted a laugh, and Ruff sipped his coffee. It tasted like acid.

"Whadya mean?"

Ruff ignored the slurred, challenging voice. The bartender shrugged an apology. "Harry's had a few too many."

"Yeah." There was always someone who'd had a few too many. One reason Justice loathed saloons. Who knew what they were trying to prove? Maybe it was as he had suspected, cheap entertainment. Except people got hurt. Broken teeth didn't grow back, gouged eyes couldn't be replaced. Men died on the sawdust-littered floors of these rat-infested saloons, staring up drunkenly at the ceiling as their own blood seeped out, wondering what had happened. And to their "friends" it was only a story to be told for a few nights and then forgotten.

"Who do I see about a job?" Justice asked the bartender when he had a minute.

"Here?" The bartender spread his arms in a gesture of astonishment.

"At the mine. Who's bossing this job?"

"Mr. Connors, of course. Carson Connors. You've heard of him."

"Yes," Ruff replied, "I have." He had heard in Denver that Carson Connors was the most unscrupulous, double-dealing speculator in Colorado. His last operation had suffered a mine cave-in in which fifteen men were killed. It was said but not proved that Connors's use of cheap materials was responsible for it.

The question in Ruff's mind was what the connection might be between Carson Connors and Siringo. Maybe none at all, he thought ruefully. He sipped at his coffee and turned it over in his mind, half listening to the murmur of voices behind him.

All he truly knew was that Amos Diggs was heading this direction. He did not know that Diggs was still with Siringo. Did not know that this particular silver strike was Diggs's objective. The trail was growing painfully convoluted.

"Whadya mean you want to work in the mine?"

A hand fell on Ruff's shoulder, and he sighed

inwardly. He really didn't need this after a hard ride in the cold, with Siringo on his mind. He turned to face the miner.

"Just looking for a job, friend," Ruff said. "Let me buy you a drink."

"Whadya mean you want to work in the mine? You!" The man guffawed loudly, snorting through his nose. "Friend, you wouldn't last a damn day underground."

"Well," Ruff said softly, "I need a job. Thought I'd give it a try."

"You!"

Ruff rubbed his forehead in frustration. He looked at the miner, a head taller than he was, and much wider. The pattern was so familiar as to be nearly boring. He was drunk. He wanted to prove something. The more Ruff backed down to him, tried to placate him, the more the man bored in with strutting confidence.

"Friend," Justice said, "I'll buy you a drink. If you don't want a drink, go on over and talk to someone else. I'm just plain not in the mood for it."

"You'll get in the goddam mood," the big man exploded. Harry looped a windmill right at Justice, and Ruff, who knew that nineteen out of twenty times that was exactly the punch barroom brawlers tried to land first, was ready for it. He stepped inside the blow and dug his own right into Harry's midsection. The miner oofed with pain and stepped back.

He grunted and shook his head like a big buffalo. Then, grinning toothlessly, Harry pushed his sleeves up and came in. He tried a right and a right again. He tried to hook Ruff's heel with his boot and shove him to the floor, where he would undoubtedly try to stomp Ruff to pulp, but Justice was too agile for him. Ruff drove a knee up, missing Harry's groin as the big man crossed his own leg over, but it glanced painfully off the miner's thigh and he roared with pain or anger.

"Balls!" the bartender bellowed, grabbing for his whiskey bottles. It was too late. Ruff was too slow getting out of the way of a meaty fist and he was banged backward into the crate of bottles. Glass shattered and whiskey seeped across the floor.

Ruff shook his head and started to rise. Harry slammed a whiskey barrel aside and moved in. Behind the big man the saloon patrons stood watching. Ruff heard their shouts urging the big man on.

Harry, eager to please the others, came in too quick. Ruff's boot shot out, catching Harry at the waist. Ruff's flexed leg straightened again like a mammoth spring, and the miner was hurled back against the bar, which collapsed as the bartender moaned.

Justice came to his feet, hair in his eyes, and he started jabbing. Harry tried to swat the straight lefts aside, but it did no good. Justice's thrusts were like rapiers, slicing through the miner's defenses. Harry's head was rocked back time and again. His nose had begun to spew blood as Ruff bored in, still jabbing, throwing an occasional hard right.

One of those rights glanced off the big man's shoulder, a second was blocked by a hastily thrown-up forearm, but the third, short, chopping, landed cleanly on Harry's cheekbone, splitting it, and the miner staggered on his feet like a stunned ox.

Harry didn't go down, however. He covered up, fighting out of a crouch. Justice could see the man's face, streaked with blood, dark with anger. Harry was no longer drunk and he was a lot more dangerous.

A knife materialized in the miner's hand, and Ruff backed off a step, then came in, kicking out with his left foot. The heel of his boot caught Harry's wrist cleanly. The sound of bone cracking was audible across the room. The big man clutched his forearm and bellowed with pain.

Still he came in. His pride spurred him on, though he seemed to know already he was whipped. His dark eyes seemed confused now, confused but still determined, and he kicked out savagely at Ruff's kneecap, trying to break it. Justice stepped aside smoothly and his own leg came up, catching Harry's on the calf. Harry's own motion carried him through, past his balance, and he toppled, landing heavily on his back, the breath whooshing out of him. He played his last card.

The miner clawed as his holstered Smith & Wesson .44, but Justice was already on top of him. One hand clamped around Harry's wrist. The other held the tip of his bowie knife against the miner's throat.

"It's time to call it off, Harry," Justice panted. As he spoke he jabbed the needle-sharp point of the bowie under the jawbone of the miner. A tiny drop of red appeared, trickling down Harry's throat.

"Time to quit," Ruff repeated, still holding the hand which rested on Harry's pistol.

"All right," the miner puffed. "All right." The savagery had leaked out of him, and he lay on his back staring up into the cold blue eyes of Ruff

Justice, only a big, bulky, and frightened man. His hand came away from the gun, and Ruff sat back, watching Harry closely for a minute, reading those eyes before he stood and backed away, bowie still in his hand, wiping back his hair.

The gunshot behind Ruff sent him in a long dive toward the overturned barrels. He drew his own Colt and cautiously stood as he realized it was over.

On the floor near the door was a rail-thin man with a handlebar mustache, dead as Caesar. In his hand was an unfired pistol, the hammer still drawn back.

Across the room a short, round man in a brown coat and derby hat was calmly reloading.

"He was about to drop you," the small man said, his eyes twinkling. "Hope you didn't mind me taking a hand."

Ruff holstered his gun and looked around the room. The miners were returning to their conversation, indicating by their lack of interest that it was all over.

"You make enemies easy," the small man said. He gestured Ruff toward his barrel table. Justice sat on the crate which served as a chair and eyed this little cherub with the shooting eye. Red-cheeked, without a hint of beard, he had small, bright eyes which seemed to hold good-humored cynicism.

Several miners were taking the dead man outside. Through the open door Ruff could see that a soft rain was still falling from the dark skies.

Harry had steeled himself with another drink and was now walking to where Ruff sat.

"Guess I got a little drunk, friend," Harry said,

sticking out the ritual hand. Ruff took it, fulfilling the convention. "Buy you a drink?"

"I don't drink," Justice told him.

"If I'da known you were a friend of Kip Dougherty's I wouldn't have started up at all," Harry said. Ruff glanced at the small man, who was still smiling, almost shyly.

"How about your friend?" Ruff said, nodding to where the dead man had lain.

"God's my witness, mister, I don't even know who the man was." Harry held up the palm of his hand sincerely. "That's not my way. Maybe I don't fight good, maybe I don't fight fair. But I damn sure fight my own battles."

Ruff tended to believe him. He watched as Harry waddled away and was embraced by his drinking partners. Ruff turned and folded his arms. "You, I suppose, must be Kip Dougherty," he said.

"Yes, sir." The small man smiled. "Kip Dougherty." He was extremely self-effacing, unusual for a man in this part of the country. If Ruff had known as much about Dougherty then as he was later to learn it would have struck him as more astonishing.

"Lawman?" Kip asked casually.

Ruff smiled. "No. What makes you think that?"

"I've seen a few. I've been watching you since you came in. I saw the way you searched the room, the way you stood. Killer?"

"No, I'm not a hired gun." Not in that sense.

"Then you're on the other side. Badge or no, you're looking."

"Maybe," Ruff replied. "Ah, you were a lawman?" he asked Kip.

"I have been. Most towns don't like the way I work."

"No?" Ruff was still trying to find a trace of a lawman's toughness in this smooth-faced rotund man. But then he had seen Kip's work. There was one would-be killer evicted from this life to Kip's score.

"No, sir."

"They call me Ruff," he said, interrupting. "Ruffin T. Justice."

"Do tell!" Kip raised a thin, pale eyebrow. "Heard of you, Justice. There was quite a fuss last time you were in Leadville."

"That was a long time back."

"Maybe so. Folks haven't forgotten it, though."

"You said you used to be a lawman. You're not the town marshal here, I take it."

"No." Kip Dougherty laughed, a merry little chuckle that was almost elfish. "They don't want law here, Ruff. Most places the people don't. It's all talk, you know. If they wanted law and order, they'd by God have it. What they really want is to do what they damned well please but not let the other guy tread on their toes. It's the sort of attitude that chased me out of the law business."

"What happened?"

"Well, sir," Kip said, leaning back, hooking his thumbs into his vest pockets. "I tended to think the law ought to apply to everyone. Most towns it ain't so, and that's not what they intend when they hire you on. I wasn't cut out for that selective law enforcement."

"You stepped on someone's toes," Ruff suggested.

"You might say that." Kip smiled.

Ruff got the idea that Kip himself was looking

for someone, but he didn't ask flat out. If Dougherty wanted him to know he would tell him; if not it wasn't his concern. He had his own bears to wrestle, and he meant to get on with it. Maybe Dougherty could be a help.

"Know where I can find Carson Connors?" Justice asked.

Ruff wasn't prepared for the reaction the question got. Kip Dougherty went rigid. His pink face flushed to crimson and he flipped back his coat skirt to reveal his holstered pistol.

"Connors, it it? And I had to save your neck. Maybe, Mr. Ruff Justice, I made a big mistake in letting you live."

7

Ruff sat staring at the man across the tiny table. Dougherty was primed and ready, and just now those merry little eyes weren't so merry, and Ruff had a glimpse into the depths of the man. He had steel in him. Now Justice could see what had made this one a feared lawman.

"Easy, Kip. What's eating you?"

"Carson Connors. What do you want with him?"

How much could he tell Dougherty? He didn't know him that well, and Ruff decided to stick with his story. "Heard he's boss on this job, Kip. That's all. I want a job."

"You do, do you?" Dougherty's eyes were still cold. "Doing what? I heard Connors is bringing hard men in, Justice, but I didn't think you would be one of them."

"Wait now, back off, Dougherty. I think we'd better get this all ironed out. I want a job. I want to meet Mr. Connors, that's all."

"Meet him," Dougherty said tonelessly.

"That's right. I had the notion that maybe he's not who he's pretending to be. Do you know Connors?"

"Yes," Dougherty said, "I know him. Too damned well I know him."

That killed that. The idea had been developing in Ruff's mind that Siringo had changed his name and surfaced as Connors.

"I know him and he knows me, Justice. He can bring in all the hired guns he wants. It won't stop me. If that's what you're here for, you'd best just turn away and back off. I'll gun you as quick as any other tough working for Connors."

"Hold it," Justice said. He shook his head and smiled. "One of us is jumping to too many conclusions, Kip. I didn't come here to hire on as a gunfighter. I never heard of Connors until I hit town today."

"You expect me to believe you came in here to work in the mines?" Kip said. He was smiling again, but it wasn't particularly nice to see.

"No." Ruff put his hands flat on the table. "I'm going to have to lay it out for you, Kip. I'm not interested in Connors at all, at least I don't think so. I'm looking for three men. Men it appears Connors has hired." He went on to the story, laying out the background of Siringo and his gang as Kip Dougherty watched and listened, nodding slowly from time to time, his expression losing its belligerence.

"Yes, that's the type of man Connors would look for," Kip said when Ruff had finished. "The bastard. All right, you've been honest with me, now I'll tell you exactly what I'm doing here. I want Connors. I'll take him any way I can get him."

"Why?"

"Why?" Dougherty allowed himself a small smile. "Damned if I know, Justice." He removed his derby and ran a hand through his thinning hair. "This is how it was," he said, folding his arms on the table. "You ever hear about the Golden Lena Mine?"

"I did." That was the mine Connors had been running, the one that had caved in. "Fifteen men."

"That's right. Fifteen men were killed because this bastard had them going deeper and faster than they had any right to go. They were blasting recklessly, timbering up with apple crates. The Lena was seeping water. It shouldn't have been worked at all, let alone the way Connors was going at it. It was criminal negligence, and I had the proof. Depositions of a dozen miners, the testimony of the best mining engineer in this country that what Connors did was criminal."

"Selective law enforcement," Ruff said, recalling what Kip Dougherty had said earlier.

"That's it. Fifteen men. Well, you see it in the paper and it doesn't strike home. 'Fifteen men killed in mine tragedy.' I couldn't touch him. The case was thrown out. Fifteen men! You see, there's something sacred about these things. No one is ever responsible. I thought to myself at the time, what would the reaction of the town have been if Connors had gone into the center of Main Street and started emptying a gun at everyone he saw, killing fifteen people? They would have boiled him in oil, torn him apart like a pack of dogs. Not a week earlier we had a lynching because some drunk cowhand trampled an old woman with his horse. But Connors had gotten away with murder times fifteen.

"Well, I couldn't keep my damned mouth shut. I was fired. I kept after him, writing letters to every bureaucrat I could think of. Nothing. It started to boil in me, Justice. I visited the widows and the kids those men had left behind. You know Connors did nothing for them? Nothing at all. He simply moved on."

"Did he come after you?"

Kip Dougherty laughed. "Three times, Justice. I was lucky."

No one was lucky three times against hired killers. Dougherty was simply very good. Now he was here, and he still wanted Connors's scalp.

"Seems we got a common cause of sorts," Ruff said. Another scuffle had broken out in the saloon, and Ruff turned his head to watch the brawlers for a moment.

"The question is, what are we going to do about it?" Dougherty replied. He got to his feet. "Come on upstairs. I've got a room. They haven't gotten the windows in yet, but it'll give us some privacy."

The fight was spreading, moving toward them, and Ruff rose to his feet as well. He followed Dougherty outside, then around to the flanking alley where a staircase climbed to the second floor. The stairs had no rail, and as Kip had said, the upper floors had no windows. Perhaps they never would have. By the time glass arrived from wherever it had to come from, the town itself might be dead. It had happened before.

Ruff instinctively trusted Dougherty, but still he let the small man go first up the stairs, through an ill-fitting door and along a dark hallway to the end room.

Dougherty led the way into the room. Justice saw a blanket had been hung across the window.

Kip lit a lamp and propped a chair up under the doorknob. No lock had been provided.

"Sit down." Dougherty gestured to the bed, and Ruff sagged onto it.

Kip kept his coat on. Finding a cigar, he lit it at the lamp and then leaned against the low bureau, arms crossed.

"Your way won't work," Dougherty said. "You'll never work your way in as a miner. Even an imbecile like Harry knew you were no miner, never would be. You don't look the part. Show up before Connors's mine boss and you'll not only be shown the door, you'll plant suspicion. If your description is mentioned around enough, someone'll put a name to you. Ruff Justice is well enough known. Siringo will put two and two together quickly."

"You're right," Justice agreed. "At the time there didn't seem to be another workable plan. There still doesn't," he added. "I wanted to see for myself if Connors was Siringo. You say he isn't."

"No. I've known Connors for five years. Slim, very debonair, narrow mustache. A ladies' man. Doesn't fit Siringo's description at all. Besides, as I say, I know where Connors has been, and it's nowhere near Dakota."

"Where in hell is he *now*?" Ruff asked. "Where is he, where is Siringo?"

"Beats me," Kip said with a smile. "Connors is supposed to be in the mine office or the adjacent house. Come here."

Dougherty gestured, and Ruff followed him to the window. The ex-marshal drew aside the blanket which hung over the window and jabbed with his cigar toward the mountain slope across the creek.

"That's the mine office. You can see one lantern lit."

"Connors isn't there?"

Kip shrugged. "I haven't seen him. There's a dozen guards along that slope. Wire and barricades. I've spent days watching from this window with no luck. As far as going up to find out—well, it can't be done."

"No?" Ruff was thoughtful. Kip glanced at him with apprehension.

"You can't be thinking of that."

"Why?"

"Man, there's an army up there."

"Guarding what?" Ruff Justice asked. "Armies aren't posted to watch over empty buildings."

"I don't know. It's too many men for the job. The richest mine in the world is relatively secure from thieves. Christ, you'd have to use a pick, and most crooks are allergic to that particular implement."

"Yes, they are, and if the strike were rich enough to be paying a hundred dollars to the ton—and not many are—that's a lot of burlap sacks full of ore."

"Then I was wrong, it has to be Connors," Kip said, gesturing with open hands.

"Or Siringo." Ruff stood and crossed to the window himself. "I'm going to have a look anyway."

"Tonight?"

"It's the only time. Now. The clouds are covering the moon. With any luck it'll start to rain again. The guards will be staying close to shelter or to a fire."

"They won't hesitate to kill you," Kip said.

"No." Justice smiled, letting the curtain fall back across the window. "I guess they wouldn't hesitate a second."

"When are you going?"

"After midnight. Let the town quiet down, the guards grow sleepy and cold. Then I'll have a look. I want to know just what is worth guarding up on that mountain."

"If it's Connors," Kip said, and now his face was dead serious, "I want him, Justice."

"You've got him. I've got three men on my list. No sense adding more. I won't interfere with your work. Connors is yours."

Kip wanted to go along, and they argued about it for a while. Ruff insisted that it was a one-man job, that there was less chance of being seen that way. The truth was, looking Kip Dougherty over he could see the man was in no way suited for this work. He was not a climbing, scrambling sort of a man. In the end Ruff won out and they settled in to wait.

The lamp was extinguished, the blanket taken from the window, and they sat in the darkness of the hotel room, staring at the dully glowing yellow light against the black mountain slope.

It was nearly one in the morning when Justice stirred.

"Now?" Kip asked.

"Yes." Ruff stood in the silence, listening. The town was still, the night pitch-black. It had begun to snow lightly. He had a hard, cold night's work ahead of him.

He went out into the hall and slipped down the stairs to stand in the alley, watching and listening. Circling the building, he found his gray horse, which seemed bitterly annoyed with Ruff for leaving it standing.

Ruff swung aboard and walked the gray into the gloom of night, crossing the creek a mile upstream from the mine road. He rode into the deep willow brush fronting the creek, letting the gray pick its way. Whatever noise they made was covered by the howl of the north wind.

Ruff again deserted the gray, leaving it tied to the willows as he looked upward, scanning the mountain slope for a way up. He intended to make his climb here, a mile from the mine entrance itself, and then work along the face of the mountain toward the mine office.

It was going to be a long, miserably cold night, and he knew it. He placed his hat over the saddle-horn, loosened the gray's cinches, and set off with unhappy determination.

He scaled five hundred feet of sloping, muddy hillside quickly, working blindly as the darkness, now nearly complete, shielded his progress from the eyes of the watchers. He had a general idea of the lay of the land, but dozens of times he stepped suddenly into a drop-off, found that he had to scramble around a rocky ridge, felt himself sliding away as the bit of brush he was clinging to uprooted itself from the rain-saturated soil.

The rain began again, falling gently through the night, changing to damp snow as the night wore on. Ruff crept along the mountain slope, once turning his back to look out toward the town far below where only a dozen winking lights, no brighter than fireflies, burned.

The wind drifted his hair across his face. His fingers were numb and raw, his muscles cramped stiff. But ahead, through the darkness, the falling snow, he could see his objective. A small rickety shack where a single light burned, where an answer—or death—lay.

Ruff leaned back against the ice-slick granite boulder behind him and checked his Colt's action. Then, grim determination setting his features into a mask, he started toward the beckoning light.

8

He clawed his way up out of the muddy gully to find the first strands of barbed wire. He tested it and found it taut. Wriggling underneath, Ruff's eyes flashed about him, watching for the first indication that he had been discovered, but there was nothing.

Nothing.

No sound but the wail of the wind, the pounding of his own heart. He got to his feet and moved in a crouch across the slope. A shadow suddenly appeared, a silhouette separating itself from the general darkness to take on the characteristics of a man, and Ruff hit the ground, his Colt filling his hand.

But the night was too dark, the cold too numbing, and the guard walked past, shoulders hunched, without seeing the intruder nearly at his feet.

Ruff let the man merge again into the night, and then he rose, creeping toward the mine office and attached house which cut a blocky outline against the starless night sky.

Justice slipped beneath the piling-supported mine office and hunkered down. From somewhere not far away he could hear wind-muted voices. Finally he managed to pick them out. Two men standing inside the mouth of the mine shaft a hundred feet upslope from where he now waited.

Ducking lower yet, Ruff moved uphill, angling away from the mine shaft's entrance. Unwilling to come out into the cutting wind, the guards were soon out of Ruff's angle of vision.

Justice took momentary shelter behind a jumble of crates. There was a light in the house, none in the mine office. There was also an uncurtained window, and Ruff looked uphill, calculating.

By circling above the mine entrance he should be able to obtain a vantage point allowing him to peer down into the house. To do so would require him to pass directly above the watching guards, yet it seemed his best chance. To try approaching the front of the house directly would again place him in the guards' line of vision . . . and their line of fire.

Ruff climbed higher yet, moving as softly as a big cat. The snow had abated, but the wind continued to rise. Justice's boot went out from under him, and as he went flat on his face he heard the mud and stone slide toward the mine entrance. Someone grumbled a curse.

"What's that?"

"Mud, you idiot, what do you think?"

"No need to get mad."

"I got enough cause. Standing out here all goddam night."

"Better take a look up on that slope," the other guard suggested, and Ruff tensed, his hand going to his belt gun.

"What for?"

"Something made that mud slough off."

"Yeah. The rain. Ever hear of gravity?"

Their voices faded away for a while. Apparently they had stepped into the mine itself to hold their discussion.

Ruff waited, pressed against the dark and muddy slope, the wind gusting across his body, chilling him.

"Who the hell . . . anyway?" The voices drifted in and out, bent and distorted by the whipping wind.

"Yeah, well, I need this job. My . . ."

"Go on up then, I don't give a damn . . . guarding anything anyway . . . back to Denver."

Ruff waited for half an hour, but no one came. The older, wiser hand had prevailed, apparently. What was it he had said about not guarding anything? No one paid men to guard nothing. Possibly the guard just hadn't been let in on the secret. What secret? Ruff's reasoning was cold and stiff with the weather, as stiff as his body, which now crawled forward the last few yards to where the vantage point lay.

He could suddenly see into the window. He could see into it, but make nothing of it. He frowned, completely puzzled.

The house, as much of it as he could see, was deserted but for two men who lay sprawled on the rough wooden floor, whiskey bottle between them.

Both men were Ute Indians.

Justice could make nothing out of the situation. They had no business there. Where was Connors? Siringo? Why the guards?

Ruff settled in to wait. With his shoulders hunched against the wind he sat the dark outcropping on this inclement night, awaiting the return of Connors, some indication of what was going on around here—here on this isolated mountain where the cold winds blew and the Windwolf prowled.

The hours slid past, the snow falling intermittently. Ruff glanced toward the skies. He could see no stars and therefore could only guess at the time, but he decided he had to go—having learned nothing. He couldn't be caught on that ledge when the eastern skies began to gray.

As cautiously as before, much wearier, he crept his way down across the mountain flank to where the gray waited. He was across the creek and back into the nameless town before dawn. He dragged himself up the stairs and into Kip Dougherty's room. The little man, who had been dozing in the chair which he had placed near the window, spun around as Ruff entered, muddy, cold, scratched, and bruised.

"Justice." He rose expectantly, rubbing his red eyes.

"Nothing," Ruff had to tell him. "I didn't see Connors, Siringo, or the others. I don't know where in hell they could be." Briefly Ruff described the night's foray.

"Why the Indians? Were they prisoners?"

"I don't even know if they were alive or dead. Dead drunk is my guess."

"Well—" Dougherty waved a hand in the air, gesturing the futility he felt. "There's nothing to do but sit and wait, then. Our alliance is a bust, it seems. I know Connors will show up eventually. He has to—this is his show. You don't even have that kind of guarantee about Siringo."

"No." Ruff yawned massively. He couldn't remember the last full night's sleep he had had.

"And I won't sit and wait. As you say, I guess we're a bust as a team. Maybe we're barking up the wrong tree, I don't know. We haven't got any proof that Connors and the Siringo gang are tied up in this . . ." Ruff's sentence broke off as he yawned again, the tears coming to his eyes. "One thing, Kip, if you don't mind. I'd be almighty grateful if you'd stable my horse and let me sleep in this bed."

Kip Dougherty grinned. "All right. There's only the one stable. Your horse will be there. Me, I'm going out to poke around. Get some rest."

Ruff intended doing just that. He already had his muddy fringed boots off, and he waved feebly to Kip as the man went out. Propping the chair under the doorknob again, Justice stripped off his shirt and pants and stretched out naked on the bed, his fingers wrapped around his Colt.

His dreams were strange rambling things. There were the flowers again. Those which always came to him in dreams. Fields of golden poppies—he always thought they were poppies—with tiny smiling faces. The headless Sioux riding the blood-red pony. Ruff pulling the trigger on his rifle. The rifle exploding in his face, the flowers lying gasping against the grass, staining the earth red.

And the woman, all bones and dried flesh, her mouth filled with cobwebs, eyes empty and leering, her arms stretched out to him. And on this night, somewhere in the distance, a great white wolf circling restlessly, a caged, crazed beast with shining eyes and yellow fangs.

He awoke in a sweat and wiped his face, staring at the ceiling for minutes on end until he recognized the room, until his tangled thoughts sorted themselves out.

Ruff swung his bare feet to the floor and padded across the room, glancing out the window where he could see dark clouds still milling above the mountains. Smoke rose from near the mine, and he could see miners and mules at work.

Peering at himself in the mirror, Justice saw he needed a shave—he had never liked going whiskered—but his gear was with his horse.

He surveyed his filthy clothing and shook his head. Snatching up his buckskins, he went to the window and shook the dried mud off. Dressing, he went out.

The main street was as muddy as ever, nearly deserted. He walked the street slowly, pausing to look into the saloon, the smith's shed, not quite ready to give up on this town yet.

By noon he was ready. He had been from end to end of the godforsaken hole. If Diggs, Siringo, and Cavett were here, they were doing the damnedest job of hiding Ruff had ever seen.

His conclusion was inevitable. He had been mistaken in assuming Diggs was heading here in the first place. And by now the man was long gone, his tracks obliterated by the storm. Ruff claimed his horse at the stable, discovering Kip Dougherty had already paid for its board and feed.

He picked up a few tinned goods at the general store which did its business out of a huge army tent, bought a fresh box of .44s, and headed out as the clouds lowered their heads again and once more the long winds blew.

There had to be another town, another mine, another day of reckoning. Ruff had resigned himself to the long search, and he was not in bad spirits despite the cold and the recent failures.

The business at Connors's town was very odd— the guards at the mine, the two drunken Indians—but it was a problem for Kip Dougherty to solve if he could. If it did not concern Siringo, Ruff couldn't take the time to study it more deeply. Still it nagged him as he rode, and he pondered it in puzzlement.

The tracks broke off his thoughts.

Very fresh tracks, and there were many of them. He was at a small creek crossing, a silver margin between two opposing armies of tall pines. Ruff let his gray drink while he prowled along the bank of the creek. There were hundreds of moccasin prints one on top of the other. He estimated two dozen men had made them. There were also the tracks of three horses, two of them unshod, one wearing shoes.

The tracks didn't belong to the horse Amos Diggs had been riding. Unless Diggs had switched horses somewhere—and that seemed unlikely out here—then it was not Diggs who was with the Indians. Perhaps it was not a white man's horse at all. A shod horse could have been stolen.

Searching further, he found what he had hoped to find. Clearly imprinted in the soft sandy soil were three perfect bootprints.

The white man had stepped down and stood watching while the Indians drank. Then together they had all traveled upslope.

The man was not a prisoner. No one had dragged him from his horse. No one had approached him. Ruff, frowning thoughtfully, returned to the gray, tightened its cinches, and stared up the forested slopes toward the high peaks ringed with black clouds.

He had followed one man down the mountain. Now he had come across the tracks of a man going up. There was a war between two Indian tribes going on, yet this man traveled with Indians.

One man coming down the mountain. Diggs. One going up. Siringo?

Ruff walked his horse up the trail, veering into the timber at the first opportunity. He rode cautiously, knowing that any man he met must be an enemy. The clouds were parting and patches of brilliant blue sky showed through. He heard the sound of falling water, and, bending low, peering through the trees, he saw a magnificent pencil-thin waterfall plummeting from a rocky ledge. Jays squawked in the pines, hopping from bough to bough, following Justice along.

It was a beautiful and peaceful scene, but Ruff was not lulled by it. Somewhere ahead the war awaited. The war and a white man who had no business here.

He found their camp by accident as dusk purpled the skies. The gray's ears went up and the horse glanced southward. Ruff instinctively reined up, resting his hand across the horse's muzzle to keep it from nickering.

Leaving the horse ground-tethered, Ruff took his rifle and moved through the trees in the failing light. He heard the murmuring of low voices long before he saw anything. Advancing, he found them. From his belly Ruff peered down into a pine-ringed clearing where twenty Utes sat having their evening meal. There was no fire, indicating to Justice that they expected trouble. The white man sat apart from the others.

Ruff tried to make out the man's face, but in the shadows it was difficult until, answering some question from one of the older warriors, he turned his head to profile.

Aquiline nose, slightly pointed chin, the shadow of a narrow mustache. He fit none of the descriptions. Not Siringo, certainly not Diggs, not Cavett. There was something . . . then Ruff had it. He hadn't seen the man before, but this one, whoever he was, certainly matched the description of Carson Connors.

That solved nothing. What would the mine boss be doing up here with a band of Utes while his silver strike operated unsupervised?

Ruff had been counting heads subconsciously, and now he realized that there were at least four men missing from the camp. Of course there were—there had to be guards out!

Cursing himself for a fool, Ruff got to his feet, eyes darting around him. He returned swiftly to his horse, rifle carried low, ready to fire.

He nearly made it. He was in time to see the Ute beginning to lead his gray away and simultaneously the second Indian pop up from behind a clump of scrub oak and cut loose with a rifle.

9

Ruff hurled himself to one side, the roar of the rifle ringing in his ears. He scrabbled for the shelter of the nearest tree as a second bullet plowed a deep dark furrow in the ground near his hand. Ruff rolled to a sitting position, fired back, then scrambled on without stopping to score his shot.

It must have missed, because the Ute continued to fire. He wasn't experienced with the weapon or Ruff would already have been dead. But he knew how to burn up cartridges. Working the lever at a furious rate, he emptied the needle gun in Ruff's direction. Sixteen shots, and they rang all around Ruff, tearing great chunks of bark from the pine as he waited his chance, the big Spencer in hand.

The Winchester fell silent and Ruff stepped out. His .56 boomed twice. There was a scream from behind the oak brush and another as the man holding the reins to Ruff's gray was blown backward, the gray dancing on its hind legs, eyes wild.

Ruff had taken one step toward the horse when the guns from behind him opened up. He whirled to see them rushing at him through the pines, and he took off at a dead run after firing two slowing shots in their direction, both without effect.

The gray, excited by events, by the gunfire, continued to prance and move away, and Justice had to abandon the animal to run through the forest.

Justice moved through the pines, his breath coming in gasps. Darkness was falling, but it didn't slow the Utes a bit.

They came on silently, not whooping or yelling but flitting like ghostly shadows through the pines, making no sound until a bronzed finger tightened on the blue steel of a curved trigger and the white man's magic thundered.

Ruff fought his way into a deep thicket of manzanita and mountain sage, making as much noise as possible. Once inside the tangled brush he began to creep downslope toward the rocky ravine on his right, moving his hands and knees with infinite care, wincing each time he made so much as a whisper of noise.

He could hear the Utes now. There was an excited whispered conference, and then they opened up again, peppering the brush behind Justice with hot lead. He held perfectly still now, waiting.

The shots died down, and it was another long minute before a voice shouted in the Ute tongue: "He is not here!"

At that Justice got to his feet, trusting to the darkness to cover for him, and plunged wildly downslope, his arm up to fend off the thorny lashes of the brush.

He reached the ravine too quickly. Unprepared, he tumbled over, landing roughly on his shoulder, tearing a knee on a jagged rock. He was trying to run even before he had gained his balance, knowing that the Utes were close behind.

Reaching the bottom of the ravine, he began jogging westward, back toward the Indian camp, praying that this would be their last suspicion. He crossed over a stack of jumbled boulders and ran on, his chest filled with jagged glass as his lungs, strangled with emotion, tried to provide oxygen for his laboring body.

His boots flew across the river-bottom stones. He was leaving no tracks, no tracks which would be visible on this dark and moonless night at least. By morning light they would find, if they still searched, places where his boots had turned a rock, small smears of mud on stone. By morning Ruff would be long gone—with any luck.

He had nearly reached the abandoned camp, but it wasn't quite abandoned. Six Utes remained, and a harried-looking white man who paced the earth, pistol in his hand. Carson Connors? If it was, the bastard was up to no good again. A man going about his honest business doesn't set a pack of Indians on the first stranger he sees. No, Connors was up to something. Just what it was eluded Ruff at this point.

He wasn't going to find out on this night either. The only sensible thing to do was to keep moving, swiftly and silently. Without his horse he was in a real predicament. All of his supplies were with the gray, but, that aside, he had no real hope of making decent travel time in these mountains without it.

Perhaps the Utes, born and bred here, could run up and down these harsh slopes all day, but Justice knew enough to admit he couldn't. He slipped back into the ravine, and pausing to listen to the night sounds, worked his way westward again, away from the pursuit.

He climbed up out of the ravine as the silver moon, absent for three nights in a row, peered through the broken slabs of clouds. Justice clambered up a layered twenty-foot ledge and paused for breath, looking down along the ravine. He could see no one and judged himself safe.

Safe, but the incident had cost him much. Looking upward, he could see another fifty-foot climb ahead of him. He fashioned a sling of sorts from his scarf. It was long enough to allow him to loop the Spencer from one shoulder, however, and free both hands for climbing.

Up he went, knowing he could be clearly seen by the silver moonlight, but judging that altitude was a strong ally if it came to a second fire fight.

He threw a leg up and rolled onto the top of the cliff, turning to lie flat on his belly and look down again into the long, moonlit gorge where the silver glow made the rocks shimmer like dully shining mirrors.

He waited on his belly for half an hour, but saw no sign of pursuit, no darting shadows, no unaccountable movements of the trees or brush. He heard nothing, and finally, satisfied, he slipped back from the lip of the ledge and worked his way into the cedar and spruce forest.

The trees were thinner on this rocky slope. Above Justice a great barren outcropping jutted, moon-shadowed, stark and wind-polished.

He worked his way along the game trail which ringed the great landform, finding that it narrowed as he went, that below him as he circled to the west was a drop-off of two thousand feet or more.

The three Utes came out of nowhere, and the first one died before the war cry in his throat could be sounded. Justice fired his Spencer from the hip, nearly taking the Indian's head off. The second Ute was already on top of Ruff, his knife flashing. Justice threw himself onto his back, kicking out with his boots as he did so. The Ute was tossed over his head to land with a thud.

The third Ute was standing, rifle to his shoulder, watching. Ruff rolled to his left, drawing his Colt as he moved. The Indian's rifle exploded, the muzzle burst showing as a brilliant yellow-red rose as the bullet whined off the stone at Ruff's back, showering him with rock splinters. Ruff's Colt spoke with authority and the Ute was sent to join his ancestors.

The moccasined foot arced past Ruff's head and kicked the Colt from his hand. The Ute, knife in hand, hovered over Justice.

Lunging, he missed his mark as Ruff twisted aside, slipping his own knife from its sheath. Justice stood, back to the high-rising outcropping, bowie in hand, watching the squat, muscular Ute feint and circle, both hands extended.

The Ute slashed out, and Justice leaped back, feeling the tip of the Indian's knife catch the front of his buckskin shirt. There was no place to go. Justice had his back literally to the wall, a great wall of moon-glossed stone. And behind the Ute was the bottomless drop-off.

Justice felt an electric feeling sweep over him. It was a feeling he both feared and rejoiced in, one which had a part in making him what he was. He stood on the rim of death, only his skill with a knife between himself and the dark void. And he laughed!

He laughed aloud, startling the Ute.

Justice stood looking into the face of death, and as had happened before, he found he exulted in the moment. Why, he could not have said. Perhaps it was buried in those memories of his life before the war, in that single episode when as a young boy he had burst upon his manhood that glorious, bloody night. But he had found it, this joy of combat which bordered on madness. He had known fear and not liked it. Later he had lost all sense of it. That he knew was true madness.

He thought once he had banished this wild thrilling emotion, but it only lay lurking silently, waiting for moments such as these. The moment when a man stood before one who would kill him and he knew that this was the final test of how he had lived: how he would face death.

In moments of battle with grapeshot flying around him, or on a deadly plain, the lances of his enemies whispering death, Ruff Justice had managed to rise to the occasion with an icy calmness which awed men no better and no worse than himself, but men who had not known that this was the moment. The moment which defined life and the reason for it.

You came and passed on. You could crawl across the face of the earth in slimy darkness or stand up and face the threats of indomitable eternity. The blackness always won. The game was rigged. Yet you had to laugh in the face of the dealer and march in.

Nothing remained, nothing could. Eternity has no relevance to the state of being a man. The greatest minds are forgotten, their works in ashes. Statuary fallen to dust, great books crumbled away, empires lying beneath the sands.

But the warriors are recalled. For a time. They would speak of Ruff Justice if only around lonely campfires in desolate mountain ranges when all other conversation had failed. Then they would forget.

But damn him if they would say he went out less than a man! There is dignity in the world, in being a man, and if it can only be purchased through combat, then Ruff Justice would stand at the head of the line.

The Ute heard the man laugh, and felt a shiver creep through him, but the Ute too had been raised to honor the good fight, the courage of manhood, and he came in, his knife flashing.

Ruff parried, steel meeting steel, as he crouched and then kicked out with a boot, trying for the Ute's kneecap and then his groin. The Ute was agile and he was skilled.

He stepped deftly aside, trying to slam his own foot into Ruff's ribs, trying to cave in the bone and drive it into lungs and heart.

Justice chopped down with his knife and the Ute aborted the attack. They circled warily. The light was failing rapidly, and Justice could see only the dark muscular silhouette, the glint of his adversary's knife.

Ruff kicked out again and then crow-hopped in a step, bringing his knife up from down under, trying for the abdomen, but the Ute twisted aside and countered with a downward slash of his own knife. Ruff had to jerk his head away from the point of the blade.

Justice stepped back and felt the rock roll under his foot. He cursed as he fell, and a cry from the Indian's throat filled the air. He flung himself at Justice, knife upraised.

Justice threw up a forearm in time to block the downward stroke of the Ute's knife. With his free hand he grabbed the back of the Ute's neck and held on.

Ruff drove his skull into the warrior's face, breaking his nose, showering them both with hot blood. The Indian straddling him writhed with pain and anger and tried again to strike the death-blow, but Ruff now had his hand locked around the Ute's wrist, and the two men, tangled together, rolled over and over, coming to a halt with the Ute's head dangling over the edge of the dark precipice below them.

Locked together, chests meeting, they breathed each other's breath, felt the blood pulsing through the enemy's body, the thudding of his heart. Ruff's tensed muscles ached. His knife hovered over the Ute, and now he knew that it was slowly descending, slowly bringing death to the Ute. The Indian knew it as well, and he muttered something in his own tongue which Ruff did not understand. A curse, an acknowledgment of his skill, a prayer, a last word to a distant love?

Ruff's knife came free and he drove it into the Indian's heart, feeling the last futile struggling of the Ute's body as he died.

He stood, wiping back his hair, staggering a bit as his muscles relaxed. He found his rifle and picked it up, his eyes still on the dead. He heard them then—other Indians on the trail below and behind him—and he looked around for a way off the ledge.

He turned his eyes briefly toward the great granite outcropping, and there she stood.

He blinked and started toward her. He stopped. She was an apparition, having no right to be

there. He recognized her even in the bad light—
the girl in the meadow two days earlier, the one
attacked by three warriors.

Now she stood, staring. She watched him from a
recess carved into the face of the outcropping,
watched him with startled, fixed eyes. Then her
head turned toward the sounds of the approaching
Utes.

"Come," she said, her hands stretching toward
him. "Come quickly."

10

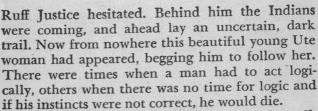

Ruff Justice hesitated. Behind him the Indians were coming, and ahead lay an uncertain, dark trail. Now from nowhere this beautiful young Ute woman had appeared, begging him to follow her. There were times when a man had to act logically, others when there was no time for logic and if his instincts were not correct, he would die.

Ruff followed his instincts. He had, after all, saved the girl from the three warriors. He had to trust her.

"Which way?" Ruff looked up and down the trail, seeing nothing but the long valley illuminated by the coming moon.

"Here." She beckoned. "Hurry!"

She withdrew into the notch in the granite cliff, and Ruff cautiously followed. Someone reached out for him, and he started to react violently before he realized that the small hand closing around his was the woman's.

"Follow," she said, keeping her speech simple, guessing correctly that Ruff's knowledge of her language was none too good.

He did follow. They were inside a gigantic cleft in the hundred-foot-high granite promontory.

There the moonlight was only a memory. All was dark and silent. The girl halted and pushed Ruff lightly, indicating that he should go ahead. He paused long enough to see what she was going to do.

As he watched she sifted sand across their footprints, working her way backward toward him. A skilled tracker would see the deception in daylight, but at night in this crevice it would take a bloodhound to follow that trail. Ruff had heard no bloodhounds.

He had learned the hard way, however, that it was never wise to underestimate an Indian on his home ground. They seemed to be able to track by scent, to instinctively know where the prey was headed, and Justice kept his rifle at the ready as he backed farther into the narrow crevice.

The girl touched his arm in the darkness. Saying nothing, she jabbed a finger upward, and Ruff, peering up, could see a narrow ledge within reach. Farther up a lone star twinkled coldly into the crevice.

The girl squeezed his arm urgently, and Ruff, handing her his rifle, scrambled up, hoping that his instincts hadn't been whispering lies. It would be a hell of a place to be caught.

She handed the rifle up barrel first, then again sifted sand across their tracks before leaping up, grabbing the edge of the shelf, lithely drawing herself up to roll beside Ruff.

No sooner had she rolled onto the ledge than Justice heard the sounds of footsteps behind them. He pressed himself out flat against the cold stone, gathering the girl to him, his every sense alert.

A single Ute had entered the crevice, and he inched forward, eyes searching the dark recess.

Justice had one hand wrapped around his rifle and one around the girl's mouth—he didn't trust his instincts that far. He could feel her hot, rapid breath on his hand, and glancing that way, he saw her round, excited eyes.

He returned his vision to the floor of the crevice, where the single Ute, crouched forward, rifle in hand, moved still nearer to where they lay on the ledge. Ruff pressed his head against the stone and held the woman to him.

"No," Ruff heard the warrior say in answer to a question from outside. "No one." There was a pause, and perhaps seeing some sign he said, "Wait."

"We are going on. Hurry," an impatient voice called.

"Yes. I am coming." But it was a while before the warrior reluctantly turned and walked from the crevice, breaking into a jog to catch up with the rest of his party.

Ruff slowly released his breath, then, waiting until the Ute had been gone two full minutes, he let the girl go. Her eyes were not accusing. Far from it, they seemed grateful. For what, Ruff could not guess. He sat up and looked at her.

She knew too much to speak yet, and so, rising slowly, she simply nodded her head again, and Ruff followed her. They walked a narrow ledge to a spot where the crumbling wall of the crevice had formed a ramp of broken rubble. The girl led the way up, and Ruff followed. In minutes, after a quick, scrambling climb, they emerged to stand on top of the outcropping as the silver moon beamed down, illuminating the deep valleys, the sharp, pine-clad ridges below them.

"Now we will kill all the Shanaks," the girl said,

and Ruff turned to look at her in wonder. She had her fists clenched, her head thrown back so that the tendons on her throat stood taut. Her teeth flashed as she grimaced exultantly to the cloud-tossed skies. "Now we shall kill them all as they have killed us. Now that you have come, great Windwolf."

Ruff could only stare at her for a moment. Then he stretched out his hands and placed them on her shoulders. Looking into her eyes, he said, "I'm not the Windwolf. How could you think such a thing?"

"I know who you are," she answered positively. "You cannot trick me, Windwolf. I saw you come to save Dream Sky from the Shanaks. You killed them all, tore them to pieces as if they were noth-ing." Her eyes were lighted strangely. "Then later when you were gone I heard your howl."

Yes, Ruff had heard that howl too. In fact, he had *seen* the Windwolf in a moment of snowy con-fusion. He didn't tell her that.

"Look, your name is Dream Sky?" She nodded. "I am not Windwolf. I did not come to fight the enemy of your tribe."

"Back there—you killed more Shanaks."

"I had to. They were coming after me."

"Because they knew you are the Windwolf."

There was no arguing with that sort of logic. The girl believed that Ruff was the Windwolf, and that was that in her mind.

Behind him now he could hear searchers mov-ing through the forest. Dream Sky heard them too. "Come now, we shall go to my village."

Ruff thought it over. He had no urge to walk into a Ute village, and he definitely wasn't inclined to fight their battles for them. They would have to rely on the real Windwolf to come down from the sky or wherever it came from.

"Hurry," Dream Sky urged.

Ruff looked at the girl, seeing her lovely face by starlight. Her expression was anxious, trusting, determined. He started after her as she led the way through the pines. At least, he thought, he would be safe for a time. The handful of men who were following him would not attempt to strike at the enemy's main camp. Perhaps he could find a horse in the Ute village. Too, it was possible the Utes, who had eyes everywhere, had seen Diggs. They might even know where Siringo was. Ruff patted his shirt. He still had the daguerreotype to show them.

Running those reasons through his mind, he had decided to go along with Dream Sky, but he wondered as he followed her up the trail, watching the stretch of her buckskin skirt across her competent-appearing hips, watching the sleek, firm calves of her legs, if she herself wasn't the real reason he followed.

It was no short distance. Perhaps ten miles up and down slopes, the girl moving as swiftly and agilely as a young doe, Ruff laboring.

They broke through tangled underbrush and climbed stony bluffs. The girl waited for him at the top of one ragged, wind-swept bluff, and as she gripped his hand and helped him up she asked, "Why do you not travel as a wolf and not as a white man? Then we could go our way more swiftly."

Ruff started to explain once more that he was not the Windwolf, then shook his head, knowing that an explanation would not be accepted, and muttered something incomprehensible.

He stood catching his breath for a moment, looking down across the dark land. When he turned back, Dream Sky stepped into his arms, holding him tightly, her head against his chest. She looked up at him with great shining eyes.

"It is permitted to touch you?" she asked.

Ruff smiled and wiped back a lock of blue-black hair from her too-serious brow. "It is permitted," he replied. "Come on, let us go. How far is it now?"

"Not far." She was smiling as she drew away and began walking upslope through the dark timber.

Perhaps it was not far to Dream Sky, but Ruff was suffering from the altitude and the long night's exertions. His chest was tight, his legs leaden when finally they reached the village of Dream Sky's people.

It was hidden in a tangled forest of dead gray trees set up against the face of a towering cliff which protected the village on that side. Around the perimeter were dozens of watchers. Ruff saw them flitting through the moonlit jumble of trees, following along.

The village was dark, poor, and crude. There was no fire. In lean-to shelters the people slept or sat watching as Dream Sky led Justice into the Ute camp. Even in the darkness Ruff recognized that many of them were injured. Children cried out from hunger. Warriors moaned with pain.

They were a harassed and beaten people. Estimating their numbers, Ruff decided they were less than fifty, many of these wounded. No wonder they were clutching at straws, waiting for the hand of Manitou to intervene, or the Windwolf to return. They were outnumbered, underequipped, desperate.

The Shanaks who had been chasing Ruff were armed with new Winchesters. These people seemed to have no modern weapons.

Eyes from out of the moon shadows followed Ruff and Dream Sky as they crossed the village to a small lean-to.

"You are tired. You must rest tonight. Tomorrow you will go forth and tear the throats from our enemies."

She had limitless faith, it seemed. Ruff only nodded and crept into the shelter, smelling the heavy pine scent, the fainter leather and wood smells. There was a bed of freshly cut pine boughs, a water jar in the corner, a folded blanket.

And as Ruff, kicking off his boots, stretched out on the bed, a lithe, warm young woman crept beside him.

She was naked in the night as she slipped under his blanket and wrapped her arms around his neck. She kissed him and whispered, "You have taken the form of a man, you must have a man's comfort. I know you mourn for your lost love, but I shall be silent and you can think of me as Dawn Fire."

He was still and thoughtful for a moment, then he drew her to him, his hand cupping her firm young breast, his lips touching her ear, eyelids, nose, and chin.

He placed her on her back and kissed her throat, feeling the strong pulse there, feeling her

108

quickened breath against his flesh. Her hands ran up his thighs, searching for him. Her breath caught as she found and encircled him. Her back arched involuntarily, her entire body going slack and heavy, sweet, preparing itself for him.

Ruff kissed her breasts, giving each slow, attentive caresses, his tongue toying with her taut nipples as her fingers wound themselves in his hair and her hips began to move in restless anticipation.

Ruff kissed her smooth abdomen, letting his fingers trail down between her warm thighs. She parted her legs, and Ruff, glancing at her face, saw that her eyes were open but distant, her jaw slack, her expression one of intense concentration as he moved to her.

Her fingers waited anxiously, and as Ruff rolled to her, she found him again with a deep sigh, and she positioned him with quick anxious movements.

Slowly he sank into her, and Dream Sky pulled his head down to hers, clinging to it as her hips began a long, swaying journey, as her legs slowly lifted and wrapped around Justice.

It was a long warm journey into distant, pleasurable lands, and when Ruff awoke once just before dawn he found Dream Sky wide awake, simply watching him, her eyes soft and wondering. He pulled her nearer and, wrapped in her embrace, slept until dawn.

There was pale-gray light in the skies above the mountains when Ruff rolled stiffly from his bed. Dream Sky had gone. Ruff's buckskins had been carefully cleaned. They hung now from a branch in the lean-to's wall beside his hat. Outside he could hear the murmur of voices, the constant crying of hungry children, the occasional wailing of a woman in despair.

Ruff dressed and went out, wiping back his hair, picking up his Spencer repeater.

By the cold dawn light the camp appeared more miserable than ever. He could see the drawn faces, the nearly naked weary children. A rail-thin dog snarled at him. An old warrior with both eyes put out stretched out a hand as Ruff walked past toward the campfire which sent a curlicue of smoke into the morning sky. They had three rabbits roasting over the fire. Around it a dozen older men and women crowded, trying to keep warm on this morning which had dawned on frosted meadows and wind-tormented forests.

"It is the one!" an old woman cried out. She stepped back, her hands to her mouth. Ruff turned and walked away, all eyes on him.

"Windwolf!" Dream Sky was rushing across the camp toward him, her body swaying attractively, bringing a smile to Ruff's lips. She reached him and, looking up wide-eyed, asked, "Where are you going?"

"Nowhere just now."

"You must eat before your battle," she said. Dream Sky's hands were clasped before her. Her hair was sleek and shining, smelling fresh and clean.

He looked back toward the cooking fire, where the Utes stood watching him.

"They haven't enough to share," Justice said.

"It is all we have, Windwolf. They have prepared it for you. You must eat!"

Justice looked again at the gathering, at the pa-

thetically thin rabbits roasting over the coals.
"How can I?"

"It is their gift. It is their way of honoring you,
Windwolf. You must eat . . . or . . ." Her
lips parted and she asked tremulously, "Have we
offended you? Have you decided not to protect
your people?"

The anguish in her voice tightened Ruff's belly.
He looked again around the camp. People in tattered blankets stood watching him with calm
black eyes. People who would be slaughtered for
reasons Ruff did not even understand. But die
they would, the young, the old, the women, the
men.

"Had any brains," he said in English, "I'd start
walking and keep walking. Of course if I had any
brains I'd be in Denver still." He looked at
Dream Sky, who watched him still with anxious
eyes. Slowly Ruff shook his head. "I will eat what
they have prepared for me."

And he did. Walking back to the fire, he was
seated on a beautifully woven blanket of scarlet
and white. The rabbit was served to him, and he
had to eat it as starving, dirty-faced children
watched him. But they seemed not to be jealous
of him. Their eyes were awed, their faces eager.

"Eat," Dream Sky urged. "Eat and grow strong.
Soon you must prowl the mountain slopes. Soon
you will drive our enemies from these forests and
we shall have our peace again."

Her confidence was touching—all he had to do
was go out and defeat an entire tribe of Shanak
Utes on their home ground. He looked at the
girl's adoring eyes and found that it was hard to
swallow the stringy rabbit meat.

What they needed was the Windwolf, a magical

creature who could prowl unseen, strike with deadly swiftness, demoralize and horrify the enemy. What they had was Ruff Justice, and he wasn't fool enough to think he was enough.

11

❈

Ruff had decided immediately that he needed to meet with the leadership of the tribe. He wanted to find out what their strength was, what the strength of the Shanaks was supposed to be. He needed to know what lay behind this war, how to end it, what had been done and what could be done by a creature less godlike than the Windwolf.

All the while he was cursing himself for getting tangled up in this. All he wanted to do was find Roscoe Siringo and his henchmen and get the hell out of these mountains. He had somehow gotten involved in the affairs of Carson Connors and was now expected to lead this remnant of a nation into battle.

The meeting with the tribal chieftains took place in a forest clearing not far from the camp. There the pipe was smoked and the chiefs in their tattered finery looked solemnly to Justice for his inspired leadership.

Justice spoke to them: "I must know why the Shanaks have begun this war."

"Do you not know, Windwolf?" an old man

with a seamed face and weary eyes asked. "You must know all."

"I was on the far side of the moon," Ruff said. He hoped his exasperation didn't show.

"Yes." The old man nodded with understanding. "From there you could not know. That is why you took so long to come to us."

"That is why." Ruff had begun to say something else, but his words, his thoughts were broken off by the sudden appearance of a young warrior.

He came striding through the woods, carrying a rifle-musket, his face haggard, his eyes glittering coldly. He was tall, strongly muscled, and mad as hell.

"What is this foolishness? Who is this white impostor?"

"Silence, Stone Eyes. Do you not know the Windwolf?"

"Windwolf!" The young brave threw back his head and laughed. His finger jabbed at Ruff Justice. "Why would the Windwolf come in the form of a white man? This is a trickster come to do the work of the Shanaks."

"I haven't come for any evil purpose," Ruff said coldly.

"Then why are you here?" the warrior demanded.

"I am here because I am here," Justice responded.

"You are a liar. A liar and a trickster," Stone Eyes insisted.

"Be silent!" the old man demanded. "You would offend the Windwolf! You would mock him who has come to help us?" He turned to Justice. "Forgive this young warlord, Windwolf. He thinks of Dream Sky as his woman. He thinks of himself as supreme chief. Those are two strong reasons for foolish anger. He is young and does not understand. Sit," he said, turning again toward Stone Eyes. "Sit!"

Muttering disparagement, Stone Eyes seated himself, musket across his lap, eyes raking Justice. Ruff couldn't blame the young warrior much. He *was* a fake, and if the man had been very interested in Dream Sky, he had reason enough for jealousy. He couldn't blame Stone Eyes, but he was going to have to keep a close eye on the man. There was no mistaking that glint in his eyes. He would remove Ruff quickly if the opportunity presented itself.

"The Shanaks lived in peace with us," the old chief began, "until the white men came urging them to war."

"The white men?" Ruff's attention was suddenly sharpened.

"Yes. The white men came and gave them guns. The white men came and said: 'Drive these others from their land. You will have blankets and rifles. We will have the Shining Mouth.' "

Shining Mouth? What the hell did that mean? Ruff had the feeling the Windwolf, who had been one of this tribe, would know that, and so he refrained from asking.

"Once long ago a white man came and asked us to sell the Shining Mouth, but it is a sacred place. How can we sell it? How many rifles would it take to buy this holy place? No, we could not sell."

"What was this white man's name?"

"Connors," the old chief said, and Ruff felt the whole thing fall into place, the puzzle resolve itself. He leaned forward.

"There are other white men now?"

"Yes."

Ruff took the daguerreotype from his shirt front. "This one?" he asked, handing the portrait of Siringo to the man.

"Ai! A frozen pond! Reflection of a man held captive! This, I think, is the man. Now he is older." He passed the daguerreotype to the others, who handled it reverently, taking it as some sort of proof that Ruff was indeed a magical creature to have produced this image from his bowels. Only Stone Eyes was unimpressed.

"I want to see Shining Mouth," Ruff said, standing. "It is important."

Shrugging, the old chief got to his feet, and, followed by the others, he began walking off through the pines. Ruff was closely followed by a none-too-subtle Stone Eyes, who kept his rifle-musket low, ready to fire.

It was two miles farther into the hills before they came across a nearly barren, knobby hill which was different from anything around. Chunks of stone littered the flanks of the hill. Nothing seemed able to grow on it.

Circling the landform, they came to a cleft which, although natural, had been widened by human hands. Ruff followed the Utes inside, expecting what he found.

He had expected it, but not expected it to be this vast. Someone had struck a torch, and by it Justice could see before him a vein of silver, easily twelve feet wide, which ran diagonally from the heart of the mountain to its summit. He stepped to the wall of silver and pried at it with his bowie. He had never seen anything like it. The ore could hardly be called that. It was a jeweler's vein. That stuff could be picked out of there and beaten down into jewelry without any refining at all. The value of it was enormous, not even taking into account the vast lode which must lie beneath the knoll.

"Yes," he said, "this is what they want."

Connors or someone working for him had located this place. How to get it had been the problem. Connors had offered to buy the Utes off, but they wouldn't sell. Perhaps the inspiration had come from Siringo. Siringo knew how to use the Indians. That was the method he had utilized at Benchmark to lift the miners' gold.

Reappearing here, imported by Connors perhaps, he had struck on the idea of hiring a neighboring tribe, inflaming old intertribal resentments, giving the Shanaks new rifles to assure victory.

Sure, crazy Amos Diggs had been talking about getting rich on a silver strike. There was no gamble at all about this. Justice would be willing to bet that there was nothing at all worth being called silver ore in the shaft Connors was sinking across the mountain. It was meant to cover for this highly illegal proposition. When the silver started coming out of the mountains all the speculators in Denver would merely shake their heads and kick themselves for not going along with Connors's folly.

Meanwhile, as Connors and Siringo grew rapidly wealthy, an entire people would be pushed aside, buried in the lands of their fathers, waiting for the Windwolf which would never come.

"You are angry, Windwolf," the old chief said, reading Ruff's expression.

"Damn right I'm angry," he said in English.

Fifteen miners' blood hadn't bothered Siringo's

conscience a bit. Now he was embarked on another mass murder. An entire tribe. Again Siringo
would not have to pull a trigger. He would just
sit back and wait for others to do that. Others to
kill, others to mine, and the silver to be delivered
promptly, thank you, with none of that gore
smeared on it.

Well, it wasn't going to be that easy. The
bastards would be stopped or Justice was going to
die trying. He would chop them down and maybe
hold their noses in a little of their own blood, and
if he had to be Windwolf to do it, then he would
be. He turned to the gathered, somewhat puzzled
chiefs.

"I've seen enough."

They nodded and slowly led the way back out
into the clear mountain light. Walking back
toward the village, Stone Eyes still scowling behind him, Ruff tried to figure a rough, workable
plan of attack. He came up with nothing. There
was only one way to handle this, and that was to
take it to them. To strike and remove the white
leaders of this war, to cut off the head and hope
the body would perish.

All of which was very fine to say, but led him
not a step closer to achieving that purpose.

Back in the clearing, Ruff faced the Utes across
the blanket and asked numerous questions.

"How many men have we left? How many who
can fight?"

"They have nothing to fight with. They face repeating rifles with bows and arrows."

"How many?" Ruff said again.

"Twenty."

"Twenty?" Ruff's heart sank a little. Twenty
men able to fight.

"How many have the Shanaks?"

"Stone Eyes?" The old chief looked to the young warrior.

"I see forty-fifty. I was to their camp two nights ago and saw that many. All with rifles. The white man was even then giving them bullets."

Justice tried to keep the excitement out of his voice. "You know where their camp is?"

"Yes, the war camp," Stone Eyes said with a touch of belligerence. "The village where the Shanak women and children stay is far distant. Six days' travel."

Ruff wasn't concerned with that. "You know where the war camp is, and two days ago you saw a white man there giving them ammunition?"

"Yes. I saw this. I and Fox Wind."

"Which white man, Stone eyes? Which one did you see?"

"Him." Stone Eyes pointed toward Ruff's shirt where the daguerreotype of Roscoe Siringo lay concealed. "I saw this man two days ago in the war camp of the Shanak Utes."

Ruff stood silently digesting that. He could feel his pulse lifting slightly. The end of the game was approaching. Siringo had run, but his running was over now. Now he would have to fight. He realized suddenly that the Utes were standing in a half-circle, looking at him, that they were counting on him for leadership. Except for Stone Eyes, who wanted badly to use that musket on Ruff. He took Justice for a fake, and he was right.

"What will you do now, Windwolf?"

"I want to see the Shanak camp," he told them.

"Yes, I will take you," the old chief said.

"Stone Eyes can show me."

Ruff turned and looked at the Ute, who was expressionless. The man slowly nodded, a gleam of anticipation in his eyes. "I will take him," Stone Eyes agreed.

"Meanwhile I would like your people to remain alert. Be prepared to move quickly. Maybe you could send a few men out to look for my horse." Briefly he described the animal and the place where he had left it. It was likely the Shanaks had taken it, but when Ruff had last seen the gray it had been running through the forest and it might still be wandering about.

"And when you find the Shanak camp, Windwolf, what will you do?"

Justice looked at the old chief and said softly: "I will cut off the head of this beast, old one. I will cut off its head and destroy it."

Stone Eyes, who was worthy of his name, stood glowering at Justice. He believed none of it. He did not take Ruff Justice for the Windwolf, did not believe any white man would help the People. Saying that Justice did intend to help and not lead them into a trap, Stone Eyes did not think Justice *could* do anything. What was his plan? To go to the other white man and perhaps join forces? What was that gleam he had detected in Justice's eyes at the Shining Mouth? No, Stone Eyes trusted this one not at all.

"Ready?" Ruff asked the brooding warrior, and he nodded, spun on his heel, and led off at a rapid pace toward the Shanak war camp, Ruff Justice behind him.

Stone Eyes moved in a long loping jog, covering the wooded slopes swiftly, seemingly without effort. He had no intention of stopping for rest, apparently, until Justice, after three hours of that, began walking and then finally stopped, leaning against a massive pine to catch his breath. The Ute returned, circling Justice, examining him critically.

"The Windwolf grows weary."

"That's right."

"How can this be, spirit? How can a ghost grow weary?"

"It's this damnable white man's body I'm living in," Ruff replied without smiling.

"I do not like you, Windwolf."

"I got that idea, Stone Eyes." Ruff took a slow deep breath. "You don't have to like me. You just have to work with me. We have the same objective."

"Have we?" Stone Eyes asked, his voice brittle, eyes harder than ever.

"I think so."

"If we do not, I shall kill you."

"No," Justice said, straightening up. "You won't kill me as long as I run *behind* you, Stone Eyes. I don't care if you think I'm the Windwolf or not. I don't give a damn if you like me. But we are in this together. I have no intention of letting your people down. We shall fight together—and then perhaps we shall fight each other."

"Perhaps," Stone Eyes said. He looked to the high peaks, where a fresh storm was gathering. Great gray anvil-headed thunderclouds rose into the deep blue sky, and from time to time an ominous rumble echoed down the long green valleys.

"It is time we go," the Ute said, and Ruff nodded.

Stone Eyes jogged on, but now he seemed to hold his pace down a little. Justice, running steadily behind the Ute, allowed himself a small smile.

The day seemed endless. Ruff's legs might have

been carved from granite. His feet dragged the ground and his lungs burned. He watched Stone Eyes through exhaustion-blurred eyes.

Suddenly the Ute's hand went up and he flung himself to one side of the trail they had been following. Justice instinctively did the same, and at the same moment he saw the three Shanaks appear through the trees.

They had been walking, rifles in hand, and now they broke into a run, shrill yips coming from their throats as they spotted the enemy.

Ruff came into a kneeling position, rifle ready, but he realized simultaneously that they had not seen him and that rifle shots were liable to alert the not too distant Shanak camp.

As Ruff watched, the three hunting Shanaks fanned out, moving stealthily through the timber, searching for Stone Eyes. Justice withdrew a short distance and then circled toward them.

There was a sudden flurry of movement ahead of him, and through the low-hanging branches of a pine he could see Stone Eyes engaged in combat. The two adversaries rolled over and over on the ground, Stone Eyes' knife striking out and missing, the Shanak fighting back desperately.

The second Shanak broke from the brush on Ruff's right. He wasn't thirty feet from Justice but still did not see the white man. His eyes were intent on the battle ahead of him.

Justice darted across the space between them and looped his forearm across the Shanak's throat before the man could cry out. And before he could mount a counterattack Justice's bowie was buried to the hilt below the Shanak's lowest rib, angling up, the long blade slashing the internal organs. The Shanak wriggled in Ruff's arms and then went still. Ruff yanked the knife from the body, stepped over the dead Ute, and went on.

Stone Eyes had finished his man. He stood now, blood smearing his hands and chest, looking around for the other Shanaks.

Justice saw him first. The Shanak had his rifle up and he had drawn a bead on Stone Eyes. Ruff reacted.

His bowie flashed through the air and hit with a dull, meaty thud. The Shanak dropped his rifle and looked down at the half pound of steel imbedded in his chest. Then, eyes flickering dully, he toppled over backward, dead.

Ruff entered the clearing, and Stone Eyes, looking from the dead Shanak to Ruff and back, nodded thoughtfully. Justice pulled his knife from the body and sheathed it.

If he had been waiting for thanks he would have waited a long while. Stone Eyes simply picked up the dead warrior's repeating rifle and said: "Good. We must hurry on now."

And hurry on they did, toward the Shanak camp, toward the murderer, Roscoe Siringo, the lone Ute warrior and the Windwolf at his heels.

12

They reached the camp an hour after dark, exhausted and filthy, bathed in sweat which the cold wind chilled against heated flesh.

Stone Eyes and Ruff lay on a small wooded knoll looking down at the camp, which rested on a long, nearly oval-shaped mountain valley floor. Pines ringed the valley thickly. Above, the high peaks thrust mammoth heads into the evening skies, where clouds gathered ominously still.

A dozen campfires burned across the long meadow. The Shanaks were anything but cautious on this night, but then they had no reason to fear. Their enemies were weak and underarmed, defeated to all intents and purposes.

They danced around the fires, and from time to time a jug was raised. They were growing drunk, growing reckless. Was it that they were priming themselves for a final battle or that they were celebrating already the victory they assumed to be won?

Ruff thought briefly of the two Utes in the mine office, dead drunk. Probably leaders of the Shanaks shown Siringo's special brand of courtesy.

He had purchased the Shanaks body and soul for a few rifles, a few gallons of trade whiskey.

"Do you see him?" Ruff asked Stone Eyes. The Ute shook his head.

"Before he was in that hut." Stone Eyes pointed, and Ruff, squinting into the darkness, saw a large army tent.

Was he there? Or gone again? Siringo was slippery and clever, too clever perhaps to stay around his band of drunken mercenaries with their uncertain moods.

"I've got to go down there," Justice whispered, and Stone Eyes nodded. They settled in for a long wait. Let the campfires burn out, let the Shanaks drink all the whiskey they could hold.

Justice lay silently on his belly, watching the faint eastern glow which was the coming moon, watching the stacked thunderheads above the mountains. With any luck those clouds would drift over and cover the moon. He sincerely hoped so. He had no urge to try it in bright moonlight.

He didn't want to try it at all—but there seemed no real option. He wanted Siringo. He wanted to stop this planned slaughter of an entire people. There was no time to sit around and wait for an opportunity which might never come. Ruff smiled.

How would the Windwolf handle this? Why, nothing could be simpler. Flit across the open space, tear the throat out of Siringo, and fly away to the moon. You never could find a Windwolf when you needed one.

Justice waited until an hour past midnight. The night had grown black. Heavy clouds were pasted to the sky. The wind had increased, and from time to time a few cold drops of rain fell through the pines.

He shifted and rose to a crouch. Stone Eyes nodded, and Justice handed the Ute his rifle to hold. It seemed to affect Stone Eyes more than Ruff's killing of a Shanak to save his life had. A man does not give away such a weapon. He does not leave it with a man he does not trust. He does not go away and abandon it if he does not plan to return.

All of that was spoken in a flicker of the eyes. The simple truth was that the rifle was more of a hindrance than a help in this situation. Justice took off his hat, folded it, and placed it behind his belt. Then, glancing once again at the cold dark skies, he slipped off through the pines, working his way toward the forest verge.

If there were Shanak guards posted on this night they too were heavy with liquor, perhaps asleep. Ruff, pausing at the edge of the long valley, saw no movement anywhere. But then the night was dark, and he placed no unwarranted trust in this.

He lay soundlessly watching. He could see the sleeping Shanak Utes, the tent beyond, smell the smoke of dead fires. He had no liking at all for this, but he had bought tickets to the ball and now the band was striking up.

Justice got cautiously to his feet and began weaving his way across the camp, his heart in his throat. He carried his bowie in his hand, leaving his Colt revolver holstered. It was useless in this circumstance. To fire it would be to invite his own death. He had to trust to stealth and silence, and if that was not enough, nothing was.

He threw himself to his belly suddenly. Not

twenty feet from him a Ute stirred and then sat up, holding his head. Ruff could only lie on the cold grass watching, his hand cramped around the haft of his bowie.

The Indian started to rise and then sagged to hands and knees. There was a gurgling sound and then a terrible retching. The Shanak was being sick on the grass, having discovered one of the side effects of the white man's magic water.

It seemed like hours before the Ute flopped back heavily on his blanket, hours more before his fluttering snoring began again. Justice moved on.

The tent was fifty feet farther on, and Ruff reached the shadows it cast quickly. He stood, eyes flashing, searching the darkness. He worked his way toward the back of the tent. It was a type he was familiar with. The sides were wooden halfway up, and the floor inside would also be wood. Senior army officers used these during long campaigns. Around the back he saw the dark, bulky silhouettes, saw the heads turn toward him.

The Utes did not have to look for his gray after all. It stood in a rank with three other horses, all saddled, which made no sense. Then perhaps they had simply been too lazy to do the job, to give a damn about the horses. They certainly weren't planning on moving out to the attack tonight, not with the warriors in the condition they were in.

Ruff moved softly to the gray and stroked its muzzle. His bedroll, amazingly, was still tied on behind the saddle. Quickly he untied all of the horses from the tether. His gray would stand. What the others did he did not care.

Ruff moved to the rear of the tent and paused, listening. A low moan reached his ears through the green canvas. He paused, tensing, but there were no voices, just the moaning, the pitiful subhuman sound.

Justice slit a small hole in the side of the tent and peered into the dark interior. Then, hurriedly, he slashed a large rent and stepped over the planking and into the tent.

He hung from the center pole of the tent. They had peeled the skin back from his arms and legs. His belly had been opened in three separate places. His face had had fire thrust into it, yet he still lived, and Ruff Justice winced painfully as he stepped nearer to Kip Dougherty.

The little man's eyes brightened briefly and then fell again to the miserable pain-filled depths. Ruff cut the ropes which bound him and lowered the naked, tortured body to the floor.

Kip's hands gripped Ruff's wrists with an amazing strength. He was trying to tell something to Justice, trying to plead, to ask, to curse, to explain—but nothing understandable came out. They had torn his tongue from his throat.

"I'll get him, Kip. I promise you."

Kip Dougherty's hands fell away, and his eyes closed tightly for a single moment. Then they opened again, wide with pain, with unbearable, hopeless pain. He gurgled a sound and clutched at Ruff's knife hand.

"All right. It's the least I can do, I suppose. So long, Kip. Dammit, you were a man."

Then Justice slit the jugular quickly, mercifully, and Kip Dougherty's head fell back, blood seeping across the floor, his eyes lighted with thanks until the light faded and there was only a cold, rotund, glassy-eyed thing staring up at Ruff Justice.

The big man burst into the tent, and Justice

whirled. Not fast enough—the boot exploded out of the darkness and took Ruff on the point of the chin. He was slammed back against Kip's body, his knife flying free.

By the dim light Ruff recognized the man, and he knew that Jethro Cavett meant to kill him.

Cavett was slapping at his belt gun, trying to paw it free, but there wasn't time. He had come into the tent expecting to find no one but his victim. He had found Justice, and he would regret the moment.

Justice launched himself from the floor and drove his shoulder into Cavett's chest, driving him back against the center pole of the tent, which quivered and snapped. Cavett tried to gouge Ruff's eyes. His hands closed around the scout's skull and his thumbs dug for them, but Justice, burying his face against Cavett's shoulder, drove a rib-cracking right into the big man's paunch.

Cavett, still heavy with sleep, liquor-drugged, backed away, and Ruff followed with a left which rocked Cavett's head back.

Justice was a madman. He had the burning image of Kip Dougherty's savaged body in his mind, the memory of the starving, battered Utes, and he had before him one of those responsible. He kneed Cavett in the groin, and when the black-bearded outlaw doubled up with pain, Ruff slammed a knee into his face. Cavett staggered backward, his face ashen, vomit trickling from the corner of his mouth.

Justice found his knife by stepping on it. Crouching, he picked it up and moved in. Cavett, amazingly, had recovered. He knew that he was fighting for his life, and the pain was washed away by the intense desire to continue to exist.

Ruff was equally determined not to allow it. This bastard had no place in any civilization, not in the company of men or that of wild animals. He had killed, would continue to kill until he was stopped. Ruff meant to stop him.

Cavett was all over Ruff, and he roared out with anger. Justice knew he had little time. Cavett's yell would bring help. Drunk or not, the warriors' instinct would bring the Utes from their beds at the sound of battle.

Ruff fought off a windmill assault of wildly thrown rights and lefts, kicked Cavett hard on the kneecap, and slammed his fist into Cavett's already damaged nose. The big man reeled backward, collapsing against the center pole again, and the pole gave.

It shattered and came apart, the roof of the tent collapsing as the jaggedly splintered center pole drove downward and pierced Cavett's fat belly, pinning him to the floor, where he writhed in anguish, knowing that he was a ruined man, that a slow, painful death awaited him.

Ruff heard the sounds of running feet outside, and he turned toward the back of the tent, fighting his way through the collapsed canvas. He slit the tent's fabric and leaped over the wooden wall, seeing men rushing out of the darkness toward him.

Damning Cavett and every mother's son of a Shanak, Ruff drew his Colt and emptied it in the direction of the charging Utes. Then he was aboard his gray, heeling it mercilessly out of there, and wild shots sang out in the night.

He didn't slow up until he was into the timber and two miles distant, until he had doubled back on his trail and assured himself that the pursuit had given up the chase. Then he stepped down and leaned against the gray's shoulder, slowly, methodically cursing.

He had accomplished exactly nothing.

The Shanaks had been alerted. Siringo was still free. Nothing had changed.

True he had gotten Cavett—if the man was not dead yet he soon would be, perhaps begging someone to kill him like Kip Dougherty—but that meant little. Cavett was only an appendage; Siringo was the head, the essential element, the fuse. And Ruff had not even seen Roscoe Siringo.

Kip must have found out where Connors had gone and followed. He could hardly have expected to find Connors allied with the Shanak Ute tribe. And Connors, Siringo, or both had allowed the Utes their savage amusements. Another good man gone and Justice was no closer to shutting down this war, to putting out Siringo's lights.

He stepped wearily into the saddle and headed southward again as the coming storm began to grumble, pale flashes of distant lightning illuminating the deep skies.

Justice rode toward the Ute camp, knowing that Stone Eyes would not wait for him after the guns opened up. Ruff would meet with the elders and try to devise some sort of plan, for the numbers of the gathered Shanaks alone indicated that Siringo was ready to begin the final battle.

The rain began to fall again, and Ruff turned his collar up. The gray horse plodded on through the cold, blustery night.

When he reached the camp it was as dark and miserable as ever. The Utes had not run. They felt an obligation to protect the sacred Shining Mouth. It was an obligation which would likely get them killed, but Justice respected them for it. There weren't many in his world who would stand up for what they believed in if the odds got lopsided enough.

There was a cry, and as Ruff rode into the camp they came out of their lean-tos to stand and stare. The old chiefs, Dream Sky eagerly running toward him through the falling rain, and lastly Stone Eyes.

"You are not dead!" Dream Sky cried. "You are not dead!"

The old chief was grinning toothlessly. "Stone Eyes told us you must surely be dead. There were hundreds against you."

Some perverse instinct caused Ruff to tell them all solemnly: "You know that Windwolf cannot be killed." Then he walked to Stone Eyes, who was holding Ruff's Spencer rifle. "Thank you for caring for this. You are a good friend."

Stone Eyes worked his jaw in some undistilled emotion's expression. Was he angry, challenging, jealous? Ruff couldn't guess. The Ute handed him the rifle calmly and turned away.

"Wait, we have to council," Justice said. "Tonight. It must be tonight."

"They are coming?"

"I believe so," Justice had to tell them. Dream Sky had taken his arm, and now she clung to it with both hands, her eyes turned up to his. The rain washed down, and Justice said, "May we meet—in the largest shelter."

"Yes, if it is what you say, Windwolf."

The old chief led the way to his own lean-to. It was a tight fit, but the five Ute war leaders and Ruff managed to squeeze in. The rain pounded down outside, and Ruff stared at it for a long minute, watching the silver ribbons weave changing patterns, watching the silver rivulets begin to creep across the packed earth of the campground.

"I must ask you—will you leave this place?"

"Leave it to the Shanaks? It cannot be done," Stone Eyes exploded.

"You all feel this is so?" Ruff asked. They nodded, and Ruff took a slow, deep breath. "There is only one way, then," he said, looking at each warrior in turn. "We must attack."

"Attack!" Stone Eyes was nearly choking with laughter. "Attack how? With what weapons? They are many and we are few."

"Yes, and if we wait for them here we will be fewer . . . and then we will be none. If we attack, we at least have the element of surprise. We can position ourselves along the paths they must travel. We can attack and then flee to fight again. We can whittle them away, and in time, as a tree that is chipped away at must fall, they will fall. Unless—I ask you again—you will agree to leave this place and let them have Shining Mouth."

"No! That shall not be."

"Then," Ruff Justice, the Windwolf, said, "we shall attack."

13

It was the poorest army Ruff had ever traveled
with. Ill-equipped, weary, some of them walking
wounded, many old and slow. Yet it was the
material he had to work with. He worried not so
much about these men failing him as about him
failing them.

. They had lived their lives as warriors, and they
would die if need be. When the warriors had as-
sembled, bows or old rifle-muskets in hand, faces
determined, they had had to argue with a blind
man and a man who had but one leg to prevent
them from following Justice into battle.

The Utes knew what was expected of them.
They had fought this sort of battle for centuries.
Any small mobile force can be effective against a
large, slow, and exposed army. The trouble was, it
was seldom that the smaller force won in a war of
duration. Through attrition the smaller army was
worn down until there was nothing left to fight
with.

Ruff didn't mean to let it go that far.

His intention was to strike first, to strike often.
To hit Connors and Siringo before they knew

what was happening and to get the hell out after the first strike.

They reached the Shanak camp in a day and a half. The invading army hadn't moved yet. Obviously they were waiting for something. Siringo's return, perhaps? Ruff couldn't see Carson Connors, the debonair gentleman, leading this army. That job would likely fall to an experienced soldier like Siringo.

Ruff led his people through the forest. They met one sentry, but unfortunately for the Shanak the meeting was quick and quite fatal.

After that they had the western perimeter to themselves, and Ruff arranged his men along the wooded slope. Below, the Shanaks lazed the day away—gambling, drinking, tale-swapping. Ruff Justice lifted his hand and then lowered it, and the guns spoke from the woods.

The muskets fired first, and in that first barrage Ruff saw three Shanaks go down. The rest were sent scrambling randomly. The camp resembled a maddened ant hill as the Shanaks darted for their weapons or for cover.

While the muskets were reloaded, Ruff Justice and Stone Eyes carried the battle, Ruff pouring the bullets through his Spencer, Stone Eyes firing rapidly with the Winchester he had lifted from the dead Shanak. By the time Ruff's magazine was empty the Utes had loaded their muskets, and they began firing again, not in unison now, but individually, each shot intended to score. There must be no wasted musket balls, no wasted powder.

Ruff, shoveling fresh cartridges into his seven-shot Spencer, settled behind the sights. He followed one painted, yelling Shanak as he rushed toward the knoll, touched off, and saw the Indian somersault to his death, the boom of the big .56 audible even above the staccato chatter of the muskets.

He got his second clean kill moments later. The Shanak decided to change positions, to seek better cover. That was his last mistake. A mushrooming 500-grain bullet from the big Spencer slammed the Shanak back into the campfire, spewing sparks and ash.

Ruff kept his eyes moving continually, searching for the white face. Connors? Siringo? Diggs? One of them, it seemed, had to be in that camp directing things, but he could see nothing but the advancing Shanaks.

Organized now, the Shanaks laid down a barrage of .44s, firing as rapidly as they could work the levers on their Winchester repeaters. They had achieved the woods on either flank and were now working toward Ruff's position.

Justice scanned the field once again, seeing a score of dead Shanaks. He tapped Stone Eyes on the shoulder and gestured with his head.

"Let's get out of here," Justice told the Ute warlord.

"We can kill more."

"We can kill more, but they'll close us in! Dammit, let's get out of here while we can."

Stone Eyes glared at him, fired a last round from his rifle, and then got to his feet. He shouted, and the Utes began to fall back, jogging in a ragged file toward the hills behind them.

Ruff, eyeing the cliffs which towered above the path they were following, spoke to Stone Eyes on the run.

"Send some young men up there. We can ambush the Shanaks."

Without breaking stride, Stone Eyes answered, "The Shanaks are not such fools. They will know it is a trap."

"They are angry now—they are not thinking."

"No!"

"If they do see the trap, then they will fall back and we have gained our escape. Order the men up, Stone Eyes. Or shall I?"

Stone Eyes stopped and stood, chest heaving, looking at Ruff Justice bitterly. The men, he knew, would follow the Windwolf's command. If Stone Eyes was to continue to be war leader it must be he who issued the commands.

"All right," he told Ruff. "But do not think I am your friend merely because we fight together. When this is ended . . ." Stone Eyes let his words trail off. "You, Raven Wing! Take three men. Climb up here. Perhaps there are rocks you can dislodge. If not, fire one barrage with your muskets and then retreat." Stone Eyes glanced at Ruff sharply. Justice nodded, smiling faintly. "That is all," Stone Eyes said. "Be quick."

The older warriors had already made it through the gap. Stone Eyes, watching his men clamber up onto the rocks, turned toward Justice. "Come now, we must go."

"Think I'll hang around and give them something to chase, make sure they come through here."

"You are a fool," Stone Eyes said angrily. Then, more calmly: "If you stay, I stay. I will not have it said that you are braver than I am."

Ruff Justice, astonishing Stone Eyes, grinned and slapped the Ute on the shoulder. "Now you're talking. I was hoping you'd offer to stay and help me. You are brave, Stone Eyes, very brave."

Stone Eyes spat a reply and turned back with Ruff to wait behind a fallen boulder, watching, listening, their rifles ready as the Shanaks behind them worked their way up the slope. Occasionally a Shanak rifle boomed, echoing through the trees, but they must have been shooting at ghosts. There was no enemy within half a mile.

"Here they come," Justice said quietly, and Stone Eyes heard the hammer of the white man's rifle click back.

There were a dozen at least, with more likely coming. Stone Eyes snuggled up to the stock of his rifle, waiting. The white man did not fire.

They were within a hundred feet and closing rapidly, and still Ruff Justice did not pull his trigger. Stone Eyes looked at him anxiously. Was the man mad?

They were fifty feet away. Stone Eyes could see the eyes of the hunters searching the rocks above him. Sweat trickled down the Ute's cheek. His finger trembled on the trigger of his Winchester. Was the white man going to let them walk over them?

"Now!" Justice cried out, and he squeezed off his first shot, the bullet thundering into the chest of the nearest Shanak. Already Ruff had switched his sights to the next man, and he fired again, hearing Stone Eyes' rifle boom twice, rattling his eardrums. Ruff scored a hit, then missed. Cursing, he fired again at the Shanak, who had now turned to try to flee. The .56 caliber bullet sectioned his spine, and he crumpled up like an unstrung marionette. Stone Eyes continued to fire. There were six dead Shanaks on the ground before them. The rest had taken to the woods.

"Come on. That's enough!" Ruff shouted. He placed his hand on Stone Eyes' wrist and nodded his head. Together the two men, running at a crouch, dashed for the pass before them.

Behind, the Shanaks burst from the trees, their war cries filling the air. They opened up and the bullets sang off the walls of the cliffs as Ruff ran into and through the pass, not pausing to look back.

The Shanaks, halfway through the pass now, were met suddenly by a fusillade of musket fire from atop the cliffs as Ruff's men closed the trap. The Shanaks tried to fight back, then broke and ran, but not quickly enough.

The Utes above them had loosened a massive boulder from its rain-saturated moorings, and now as the Shanaks tried to make their run the boulder was given the last push and it tumbled down, slowly at first, rolling over and over, kicking smaller head-sized rocks before it. Then the boulder gained impetus. It bounded high into the air, and when it hit again the side of the cliff seemed to come loose. Mud began to slide off and the falling rocks cascaded down into the narrow gorge.

The Shanaks who had been too eager to pursue Ruff and Stone Eyes were now trapped, and the rocks from the bluffs struck as effectively as cannon balls, crushing those in their way.

As Ruff watched, a Shanak was smashed to soup by a gigantic boulder, another knocked senseless by a dozen fist-sized rocks before the mud sloughing off the bank buried him.

But they would not stop. They would keep coming, damn them! Ruff knew it, and so did

Stone Eyes, who watched Justice without pleasure.

"Come on," Ruff said. "Let's join the others."

"We join them, and then what? The battle is not over, Windwolf."

"No. I'm afraid not. It's only begun. So let us council again. Before the night is over we shall attack again."

"Again?"

"Again and again. We will win, Stone Eyes. We will win if we continue to strike when the enemy does not expect it, where he does not expect it. If we rest, if we pause to congratulate ourselves, he will crush us."

Ruff turned and started away, but Stone Eyes put a hand on his shoulder, halting him. The Ute's eyes narrowed and he asked, "Why do you do this? Why do you fight for my people? I have thought you would falter, that you were tricking us. Now I see that you are indeed fighting for us, but I do not understand it."

Why was he? Maybe it had something to do with a strange creature which had appeared out of the snowstorm, one which dogged his tracks and howled out forlornly. Maybe he had been chosen by the Windwolf in some way—maybe he was mad. He told Stone Eyes: "You know I have taken a vow to return in time of trouble."

"You are not Windwolf!" Stone Eyes said in frustration.

"Who is to say?" Ruff replied. Then he grinned, and, turning, he jogged on to where the Ute warriors waited.

"We have won a great victory!" the young warrior called Raven Wing shouted. "Aiee! We have driven them from our lands."

The more sober warriors, the older ones who

understood the situation, looked quietly to Ruff Justice. "What shall we do now, Windwolf?"

"Attack," Ruff said, and his voice was merely a hiss issuing from between clenched teeth. "Attack again. And again."

"Soon it will be night. We cannot see to fight."

"Then they cannot see to repulse us. We shall attack tonight. This time from the rear. It means a long night's march. There is no time to sleep. Are you willing to follow me?"

"For myself," said the old chief, "I would follow you to the far side of the moon, Windwolf. My old heart is young again, for I know that I am fighting for the existence of my people. Lead us. We shall follow."

There were no dissenting voices, although Stone Eyes, who stood apart from the rest, shook his head heavily. Ruff knew what his thoughts were. These old and wounded men would now be required to run through the night, to fight a pitched battle in the darkness, and then run again to escape the superior numbers of the Shanaks. It was doubtful that they had the strength to do it. Ruff understood that, but he also believed they had to gamble, had to take the war to the Shanaks or be inexorably crushed. It was all or nothing. They would strike a crippling blow on this night or they would be defeated. That was the choice, and Ruff Justice liked it no better than Stone Eyes did. He did not believe in gambling at war, but he saw no alternative.

Or only one—find the head and sever it. Find the brain and separate it from the body. Crush Siringo once and for all.

14

They moved out again sometime after midnight when the low mist had crept its way over the mountain peaks, filling the valleys and canyons with liquid clouds, and the air was chill and damp. Ruff led the way, walking again—he had spent more time walking these last few days than in months, and he wished he had the stocky little gray mustang between his legs, but a man afoot is more silent, and that silence might mean the difference between living and dying.

They took a long circuitous route toward the Shanak camp. Ruff only half expected them to be there. Likely they would have moved on, pushing toward Shining Mouth, but his Utes were first-rate trackers and they would have no trouble following.

As it happened, the Shanaks were still in the old camp, hardly expecting the small band of Utes to return. They had, however, placed out dozens of extra sentries, and on this night they would not be fogged with liquor.

Ruff lay on the mat of sodden pine needles beside Stone Eyes. Looking through the trees, they could see the camp. No fire was lighted. The

Shanaks had made their beds in places of conceal-
ment—behind fallen logs, in depressions—and this
time there would be no easy sniping.

"I think not all are in this camp," Stone Eyes
pointed out. Ruff had to agree.

"Where? Behind us?"

"I think so. Shall I send runners to look?"

"No. It would only alert them. It's a trap sure as
you're born. At the first shots the rest of the
Shanaks will close down on us."

"Then what shall we do, *Windwolf*?" Stone
Eyes asked, managing to give the word his cus-
tomary heavy sarcasm.

If he had had a cavalry unit Ruff knew what he
would do. Ride right through that damned camp
destroying everything they saw, then out the other
side. Straight through with a minimum of casual-
ties. On foot it wasn't practical.

Something else caught his attention. He mo-
tioned for Stone Eyes to be silent. They were
within a hundred yards of the camp, the mist
hovering just above it, sometimes cutting off their
view. Just now it wasn't what Justice saw that
held his interest. It was what he heard.

Muffled, indistinct voices speaking English.

" . . . the hell out of here."

"You'll . . . I say, dammit, you're getting
paid . . ."

Ruff's heart picked up a little. Connors was in
camp. And with him another white man. Siringo?
Suddenly he knew what he wanted the Utes to do,
what his plan of attack would be.

"Bunch up along the ridge," he told Stone Eyes.
"Cut loose with the muskets—there should be time
for two shots each—then get the hell out of here.

Circle back for the village. You'll likely have to fight a running battle on your way."

"You speak as if you do not mean to come with us," Stone Eyes said. That familiar distrustful tone was in his voice.

"No. I'm not coming." The Windwolf was going to stay behind, and as the Utes withdrew, leading the pursuit away from the camp, he was going to penetrate. Connors wasn't the sort to take off in the dead of night into an enemy-infested forest. Leave that sort of thing to the mercenaries. No, Ruff was confident he would stay behind. That would be the biggest mistake of his life.

"I do not like this, Windwolf." Stone Eyes rose. "We fight, we run, and you stay hidden."

"That's the way it's got to be," Justice said.

"Yes. That is the way. If this is treachery—I shall not forget you."

"If it was treachery, I wouldn't want you to. This time, for once, Stone Eyes, trust me. I have fought beside you before, but this time it must be alone."

Grunting, Stone Eyes turned away. He gathered the men around him and whispered Ruff's instructions. Dark eyes turned toward Justice, accusing, questioning—why was Windwolf not going to fight with them? Ruff turned his head away and lay silently watching the camp as Stone Eyes led his ragged army away to the south, sifting through the pines as silently as the clinging mist.

There was no sign of motion in the Shanak camp, no sounds reached Ruff. Once, however, he saw something which interested him highly. A brief flash of dull yellow light. A wedge of color bled out onto the long grass of the meadow.

It had come from the tent. They had repaired

the center pole, dragged the bodies away, and moved back in. These were not sensitive men. A little blood on the floorboards wouldn't bother them a bit.

And they were in there now—the two white men Ruff had heard arguing earlier. He smiled and settled in, the chill the sagging mist brought bothering him not at all. They had pinpointed themselves for Justice.

The guns opened up from the ridge to the south, and Ruff tensed. There was answering fire from the camp, a shouted command. The flap of the tent opened and light streamed out for a second until a wiser head extinguished the lantern.

The Shanaks were up and rushing toward the ridge, and Ruff knew they had expected something like this. The second barrage was fired a minute later. It was difficult to see if any of the shots were scoring. The mist had draped itself over the valley, and there was nothing visible on this night but shadows, wisps of cottony cloud, dark, dripping pines.

Ruff waited still. By now the Utes under Stone Eyes should be making their retreat, and by now the Shanaks should be in hot pursuit. The fog would be an ally of the hunted; it would be Ruff Justice's ally on this night.

He rose, Spencer repeater in hand, and began to slip softly through the mist and the forest toward the silent camp below.

A stalking shadow caused Ruff to go to his belly. Connors hadn't stripped himself of all protection. Justice let the guard go by, counted to thirty, and dashed toward the tent, his boots soundless against the dew-heavy grass. The mist hung so heavily across the valley that Ruff was dripping wet, and when the tent suddenly appeared before him it was unexpectedly.

His heart, thumping from the run, now began to slow, becoming a dull, insistent thud. His eyes narrowed, and he smiled thinly. That odd battle calm had come to him, that eerie coolness which was nearly frightening in retrospect and which he suspected would one day get him killed. Justice had the ability at times like these to focus only on the objective, on the enemy; all personal fears and apprehensions were swept aside by the cold wind within. He approached the tent with utter calmness.

They would not be expecting him, and so he walked directly to the tent flap, flung it aside, and stepped into the lighted interior.

The lantern had been turned down so that the wick fizzled and sputtered, casting off no more light than a match. But there was enough light. Enough to see Carson Connors, and springing from the cot to Ruff's left, Amos Diggs.

"Who in hell . . ." Connors stammered.

Amos Diggs wasn't the type to talk, to ask questions—besides, he knew very well who Ruff Justice was. He had tried to have him killed back in Lode.

Diggs hurled himself toward the rifle which was propped against the far wall, and Justice leaped to stop him. He couldn't have any shots fired in this tent. The tent would be swarming with Shanaks in a matter of minutes.

Justice slammed into Diggs, crashing his fist into the big man's jaw. The redhead shook it off, rolling with the punch, grabbing at Ruff's leg so that they fell together to the wooden floor, shaking the tent while Connors, who seemed to regard it all as a display of bad manners, backed to the far corner.

He was involved enough to scream out to Diggs, "Kill him, kill him!"

Diggs was doing his best. He had killed a dozen people, one poor Lode, Colorado, prostitute among them. Diggs was powerful and he had done some fighting. He had Ruff beneath him, and he tried to smash his forearm across Ruff's throat. Justice, tucking in his chin, managed to escape with a glancing blow to his jaw. Ruff got his long legs up, hooked his boots under Diggs's chin, and lifted the red-haired thug over backward.

Diggs pawed his way free and got to his feet, his face as red as his hair, his features frozen and cold in the sputtering lanternlight. Reaching back, he came up with a camp chair which he flung at Ruff. Justice ducked and came in, his bowie out now, and Diggs backed away, circling the tent, while Connors continued to rave.

"Kill him!"

Diggs was doing his best to accomplish just that. From the camp equipment on the floor behind him he had snatched an ax, and brandishing it challengingly he stepped nearer to Ruff, his huge feet sliding across the floor as he sought to close the distance and maintain his balance at once.

Ruff backed up. It's a fair idea when facing a man with an ax. From the corner of his eye he saw Carson Connors grinning gleefully, his hands clasped together.

Ruff reversed his knife, and before Diggs could react he flicked it underhand toward Diggs. The big man took it in the belly, pawed at it dumbly, and keeled over, his eyes even now showing no fright. He was a brute who had walked the earth only to maim and to kill. He had never understood that he himself could be killed, and so he had never known fear. Now he was dying, slowly, a worm of blood creeping from the corner of his mouth, his clouded eyes rolled back as he gurgled some last, futile curse.

Connors made a dash for the tent flap, and Ruff threw himself in that direction, dragging Connors down by the ankles. The man fell hard, cracking his head against the floor, and when he opened his eyes the long-haired man sitting on his chest was blurry, indistinct. Gradually Connors's eyes cleared and he realized that this interloper had killed Amos Diggs, that he was very likely going to kill him. That feeling was intensified as Ruff Justice, slipping his skinning knife from inside his boot, jabbed the point of the deadly little weapon under Connors's chin and pressed.

"Where is Siringo?" Ruff demanded. His voice, surprising even himself, was hoarse and thick. Connors trembled beneath him, turning his head as he tried to move away from the blade of the knife.

"Don't move," Justice told him. "You'll likely slit your own throat. Now then, if you don't want that to happen"—he jabbed again, and the needle-sharp point of the knife bit into the slack, thin skin of Connors' throat, drawing a bead of crimson blood—"where is Siringo?"

Connors's mouth opened, and he gabbled something. There was an unhealthy odor rising from the man, and Ruff decided he had messed his pants. Connors had plenty of guts when it came to having someone else do the dirty work. Someone else torturing Kip Dougherty, someone else killing innocent Utes. He didn't have what it takes when the violence came home.

"Listen . . ." he panted.

"I only want to listen to one thing," Ruff said, pushing the knife in a little deeper. "Where is Siringo?"

"You don't understand! There's millions in this. You can be a wealthy man."

"I couldn't stand the company," Justice said. He jabbed again, and Connors started to scream. Ruff clapped his hand over the man's mouth and bent close to him.

"Connors, you've got one minute to live. You tell me where Siringo is and maybe you've got a little longer. Maybe I'll let you get out of here, and if you're fast enough maybe you can escape the hangman for a little while. Maybe Kip Dougherty's friends won't find you for months, years— but dammit, if you don't talk now, you'll die here!"

Ruff grabbed Connors by his neatly barbered hair and forced his head to one side so that he could look into the dead eyes of Amos Diggs.

"I'll do it again," Ruff promised. "Time's up." The knife bit more deeply into Connors's throat.

"All right," he gasped. "He's in town picking up supplies. More ammunition." Connors's face had turned a pale blue, and he was as slack as a sack of potatoes. "For God's sake, it's the truth!" he croaked.

Ruff nearly believed him. He knew that he had used up any time he might have had. How long would it be before some Shanak warrior came to report to the boss? Not long, Ruff was guessing.

"All right," he said. "Get up."

Justice rocked back and got to his feet. While a

stunned Connors got up, Justice tucked the skinning knife away, recovered the bowie from Diggs's belly, and snatched up his Spencer repeater.

"Now," Justice said, "let's go."

"Go!" Connors's voice shrieked. "I thought you were going to let me go if I told you where Siringo was!"

"Did you? A slight misunderstanding there. How could I let you go, Connors? A bloody little bastard like you. Come here."

Connors hesitated, but Ruff lowered the muzzle of his rifle and Connors complied. He turned his back, and Ruff gagged him with his scarf.

"Now. The horses still out back?" Connors nodded. "That way, then. Not through the flap!" Justice slashed the back of the tent open and stepped back. "You first."

Connors hesitated, and Ruff shoved him forward so that he toppled through the slit in the tent. Justice was behind him, holding on to Connors's coattails. The three horses stood watching them. Two were saddled, presumably Connors's and Diggs's horses.

Ruff threw Connors onto a horse and himself mounted, the muzzle of his rifle trained on Connors at every moment. "Now then, we're riding out of here. Eastward. Then we're going to find Siringo. If you're good, if you're lucky, you'll live through this night. Make any trouble and you'll go down."

Connors's pale face glistened with sweat. He nodded, and Ruff told him: "Ride out. At a walk. If there's trouble, heel that pony hard. If you stop, you're a dead man."

Connors turned his horse, and with Ruff behind him, eyes flashing in all directions, every sense alert, they headed eastward, away from the Shanak camp.

They nearly made it.

An overenthusiastic guard popped up from out of the mist, and seeing Ruff he fired from the waist with his Winchester. At the same time he let out a war cry, a ringing scream which echoed through the fog. Ruff thrust out his Spencer and triggered off as the .44 from the Indian's Winchester whipped past his ear. The Shanak Ute was blown backward into the mist.

"Ride!" Justice shouted, and Connors, eyes like saucers, savagely heeled his horse. From behind them the guns opened up. Ruff, looking back across his shoulder, could see the winking red eyes of a dozen guns. He leaned low across the withers of the roan he rode, and whipping the horse with his reins he followed Connors into the swirling, cold mist.

Connors was jerking like a scarecrow in the saddle. The sounds of the guns were falling away behind them. The cottony clouds closed out the view of the valley below.

"I . . ." Connors turned to face Justice, and blood spewed from his mouth. He toppled from the saddle, the horse dancing away as Connors hit the ground. Justice sat the roan, looking down at what remained of Carson Connors. He had always hired his killing out. Now one of his hired guns had come home. There was a small hole in his vest front, a gaping exit wound high on his back. He was a dead man and he knew it. He opened his mouth to say something else, but Ruff didn't wait to hear what it was.

He kneed the roan and vanished into the mist and the night, riding higher upslope until he was sure he was out of sight. Then he gradually turned the horse north, toward the nameless town with its empty mine and the bastard killer, Roscoe Siringo.

15

The mist slid down the mountain slopes. Long cottony fingers probed the dark valleys below. From where Ruff Justice now sat the weary roan he could see not only the cloudy valleys but the jagged jutting high peaks cutting stark, primitive silhouettes against the icy, starlit sky.

And far below a handful of dim lights gleamed. Justice sat watching the lights, but oddly his thoughts were not on the end of the trail, on Siringo. They were with a small band of Indians far to the south. A ragged, brave people who fought with all they had against aggression.

He did not know how they had fared this night. Perhaps they had been defeated finally. Perhaps they cried in vain to the empty skies, calling to their patron, the Windwolf, the savage and undefeated spirit of their tribe.

By now they must feel that Ruff had deserted them. He had sent them into battle and then disappeared. His reasons, logical and pragmatic, must have eluded them when the bullets started to fly and they knew only that the white man was not there to fight beside them.

None of that could be helped. It wasn't the first

time Justice had let someone down. We all let people down—friends, sons and daughters, lovers, fellow soldiers, all expecting too much of what, after all, is only a man.

Tugging his hat lower, Ruff Justice started the roan toward the lights of the distant, fog-shrouded town, the horse's hooves making crackling sounds against the frozen grass, distant voices crying in Ruff's mind.

The night was cold. Ruff's breath hung before his face. The horse steamed as it walked the long trail. The wind came up within the hour as the moon was just peeking above the serrated edges of the mountain range. The valley below seemed tossed into confusion by the east wind. The fog swirled and twisted itself into clotted confusion, long strands of mist stretched skyward from out of the forest like probing tentacles.

And with the wind came the sound. The eerie, haunting wail which was the Windwolf. It was a mocking sound on this night, and Ruff Justice turned involuntarily toward the mountains as if the wind were a tangible thing, the Windwolf a form which might be discerned on this evening.

"Yeah," Ruff muttered to no one. "I let them down, maybe, but this seemed to be the only way. Cut off the head—too damned bad if the body still had enough strength to kill."

He was five miles above the town, which nestled in the deep valley between the flanking, timbered hills. The wind shrieked in the pines. Fog drifted past, rushing like frantic twisting specters.

The man with the gun stepped from behind the tree and shot Ruff Justice.

Ruff saw several things simultaneously. The

rifle muzzle flashing red, the face behind the sights, the horse dancing away, the sheets of cloud smothering the forest, the silver moon far away. Then he felt the searing pain of the wound high on his shoulder, felt the impact as his face slammed into the earth and the roan took off at a dead run through the forest, trailing its reins.

Ruff saw the rifle spew flames again, felt the thud of a bullet digging into the soft earth beside his head.

He rolled away, his shoulder burning as if the bullet had set fire to him. As he rolled, however, he had presence of mind enough to draw his Colt and, firing three times from the hip, drive back the rifleman.

Siringo.

It was Siringo and no doubt about it. In that single moment Justice had seen and recognized his quarry. His prey. Except now the prey was the predator, the quarry the hunter.

Ruff got to his feet, clutching his shoulder, and he half ran, half staggered toward the shelter of the woods as the rifle behind him opened up again, the bullets singing around him, whining off the damp trunks of the pines.

Ruff wove through the trees, the bullets trailing after him as he ran in and out of the swirling mist.

Too many shots. That thought penetrated the pain-induced haze. Ruff leaned heavily against a tree, holding his damaged arm, staring back through the dark forest. Too many shots for one man to have fired. Siringo was not alone. Utes? Ruff hoped they were not. An Indian in the forest was too much for him to handle right now. They were too good, and his body was slowly leaking life. He didn't attempt to look at the wound. He didn't want to see it if it was as bad as it felt. Using teeth and his left hand, he hastily tied his scarf around the wound, stifling a cry of pain as he tightened it down.

A bulky shadow burst from the trees, and Ruff, still leaning against the tree, brought his Spencer up and shot the man.

He died silently, kicking his legs in a futile death run. Ruff had never seen him before. A big white man with the mark of the wilderness on him: buckskins, beaded hatband, another recruit for Siringo's army of destruction.

Ruff had been standing in place too long, and he suddenly realized it. He had to move. *Now, dammit!* His body slowly responded to his mind's urgent command and he was off and moving, loping uphill instead of down as they would probably expect.

The moon flickered through the trees. Curlicues of mist wound through the forest, clutching at the trees. The wind racketed in the pines. The rifles opened up, and Ruff threw himself to the ground, landing painfully, the red dots exploding behind his eyes.

He rolled downslope into a shallow gully, picked himself up, and changed directions again, running in a crouch up the gully, his breath coming in tight gasps, his hair thick with pine needles, his shoulder biting with pain.

Ruff saw the jumbled stack of boulders ahead of him and he zigzagged his way toward them, meaning to make his stand there. Someone else had had the same idea.

A tongue of flame lashed out toward him, and Justice fired back on the run, hearing his bullet whine angrily off the stone and ricochet off into the woods. The gun opened up again, but by then Justice was back into the heavy timber, running upslope once more.

He had to stop. His burning body demanded it. His lungs ached, and his legs, tested beyond endurance these past few days, now trembled as he slowed, walked on, and sagged to the ground to sit beneath a massive cedar where a patch of snow still lay.

Justice looked at his arm, saw the maroon stains on his shirt, felt the buckskin sticking to his arm, saw the narrow red rivulets trickling between his knuckles. It was fascinating to him, and he held his hand up, turning it over, watching the blood dribble down to spot the snow.

With an effort Ruff shook himself out of that mood. There would be a hell of a lot more of his own blood to watch if he didn't snap out of it.

Siringo had been expecting him; that he knew now. He had gone back into town to hire some more men, perhaps realizing that if Justice was caught in town the Utes would be of no use to him. Even in a setup as crooked as this, the army would come in immediately if the Utes quit warring on each other and started killing whites in the center of town.

How had he known Justice was after him? Cavett certainly had never had time to talk.

No, but Kip Dougherty certainly had. The man had been tortured for some reason, and only now did Ruff realize the reason.

Siringo would want to know who else knew of this scheme, how many men Dougherty might have with him. Poor Kip. Well, Justice imagined he would have talked himself once they started peeling the hide back, once talking became the only means of saving himself. It hadn't saved Kip, though; it never did. After you were through talking you became worthless.

Ruff's head came up with a jerk. He had been sitting there too long. He had to move.

He was suddenly aware of the cold, of the lash of the wind, of the weakness in his limbs. Still he got to his feet, using the Spencer as a crutch.

How many rounds did he have left in that magazine, anyway? His ammunition was with the gray. He saw them suddenly. Coming inexorably on. A dozen men sifting through the pines. Shadows merging with shadows, blending, then separating.

He watched them for a long moment, perversely liking the image they presented. Dark specters stalking. He shook his head clear and staggered on, moving at a stiff trot which was all he could manage, his right arm dangling limply at his side.

The sound was like thunder, a mad frenzied sound, and Ruff's head came up to see the horse nearly on top of him, the rider charging down the slope at a breakneck speed, and as Justice watched, the man fired, the bullet a near miss, amazingly accurate from horseback.

Justice went to his back and fired the big .56 Spencer. The horse, taking the bullet square in the chest, folded up and started to roll. Justice was directly in its path, and as he tried to dive aside his foot slipped and he went down.

The rider was bucked high into the air, and Ruff had a fleeting view of his teeth, of the whites of his eyes. Then the rider was thrown into a pine, and the sickening crack of his neck snapping was audible above the shrill whinny of the horse.

The horse rolled, flailing, deadly hoofs cutting the air. The ground shook as the horse landed on its back inches away from Justice, so near that he could feel the body heat of the animal. Then the horse slid away and Justice was to his feet, struggling on, knowing that he was winning the battles only to likely lose the war.

They were wearing him down with their numbers. The pain was telling, his ammunition was running low. It seemed he had been running forever, fighting endlessly in these frozen, bitter mountains.

Well, he thought, there's a way out. There's always a way for a man tired of the fighting. You lay down your weapon and you die.

He wasn't quite ready to pay that price.

The moon had disappeared into the nether regions of the skies. Dark clouds sheeted over the faintly glimmering stars let no light filter into the eerie winter-dark forest.

Ruff managed a tight smile. He could see nothing in this light, but they could not find him either. As long as it held. The weather had been constantly changing for days. Rain, sleet, snow, fog and sudden clearing.

He slogged on, moving steadily upward toward the high peaks, making use of the darkness while it lasted.

It nearly cost him the game.

The ground seemed to open up at his feet, and Justice was grabbing for something to hold on to. His groping hand found nothing. He fell for what seemed like a minute, the darkness sucking him down, caressing him softly for a fragment of a moment. Then reality returned, sharply.

The ground came up, an icy, stony fist to smash

into Ruff's body, and the world was extinguished by a wave of brilliant yellow light, by crimson sheets of pain.

When he finally opened his eyes again it was to utter darkness. The pain returned with a violent rush, and he nearly screamed out. His stomach lifted with nausea, and Justice turned his head for the inevitable.

Then he lay back, unmoving. He stared at the cold skies, listening to the harsh, discordant song of the wind in the pines.

Something cold touched his eye, and he lay watching the confetti fall for a long while before he realized that it must be snowing. It swirled down and Justice watched the patterns it formed falling to the ground.

Then Four Dove floated down, her body formed of snowflakes and filaments of golden fire.

"My husband," the Crow woman said, and Ruff smiled.

"You shouldn't be here, Four Dove."

She simply smiled, and he saw the feathers spill from her mouth. She was offering a gift which Ruff could not recognize. It seemed small, pink, and it wriggled in her arms before she poked it away into the secret cavity in her breast. She smiled again and then was gone.

"I'll come home again one day," he said, but there was no one there and the snow drifting down was lying in a thin film across his body. An ice-heavy branch cracked somewhere in the forest above, and it sounded in Ruff's ears like a harsh, mocking laugh.

He sat up suddenly as it all came home. He lay back immediately. The abrupt movement had drummed pain through his head. Now he gingerly

160

fingered his skull, finding an egg-sized lump, a scab of frozen blood, but the bone didn't seem to be fractured, although you couldn't prove it by the pain which surged through his brain.

His arm, which had lain respectfully dormant in deference to the stunning pain in Ruff's skull, now chimed in with fiery insistence. Justice had been trying to rise again but now lay back, exhausted by the simple effort, beaten down by the shattering pain.

He came suddenly alert. His head throbbed. The night left him blind. Somewhere above him someone was moving. Low voices murmured, the sound sinking down to where Ruff lay.

"See him?"

"If I saw him, dammit, you'd hear me, wouldn't you? Think I'd keep it a secret?"

"He came this way. The bastard's not a ghost. He's here," the snarling voice responded.

"Where?"

"How the hell do I know? He didn't get over this gorge, I'll damn sure wager on that." Ruff heard a stone drop near his head. "Deep," the man said dully.

"All right. Upslope then. He must have gotten across it. If he was below, they'd have him."

They walked slowly away. Ruff could hear another wind-garbled remark and then there was nothing. He lay there still, shivering.

"They'll find you," he told himself, stirring again. "Get up and get moving, Justice. Now!" The command didn't work. The body was in mutiny. It lay there, puddled against the cold stone at the bottom of the gorge.

He thought for a moment. The men he had overheard had indicated that the majority of their force was downslope. "If he was below, they'd have him," someone had said. That meant he had to go up. Higher yet where the cold winds blew. He couldn't remain where he was. With the dawn he would be visible and vulnerable. It had to be now. With sharp determination Ruff sat up. The little men with the sledge hammers began pounding at his skull again, but he fought off the pain and got to his knees and then his feet.

Orienting himself, he staggered northward—or what he believed to be northward, up the long chute of stone and rubble which was the gorge where he had fallen. Looking up, he could not see how he had survived the fall at all . . . but then he didn't feel definite about his survival yet. The pain he carried with him screamed for relief, and there was to be none.

There was still the battle, still the last mile to walk. He thought of the massacred miners at Benchmark, of Tillie, of Kip Dougherty, of the murdered Utes, killed only because they wished to protect their land, their women and children, from marauders.

There would be no relief. There would be no surrender to the softly beckoning forces of death and sleep until Roscoe Siringo himself was wrapped in the loving arms of Death.

16

····——◆——····

The storm was a howling wash of wind-whipped snow and sleet as Ruff Justice crept along the ledge which snaked its way across the flank of the mountain peak. Below, the world was lost beneath the swirling maelstrom of white. The sky itself was lost behind the opacity. There was no reality but the narrow, icy ledge, the cold wind, the roaring pain, the hunters behind who still stalked the Windwolf of the Utes.

They were still back there. From time to time a rifle shot would crease the muddled roar of the storm with a sharp crack.

The trail narrowed, and through a gap in the clouds Ruff could see the awesome pit at his feet. The mountain fell away sharply. There was a drop of five thousand feet or more beneath him, and there was no way anything but an eagle could negotiate the gorge. Above, sheer, ice-slick walls of stone rose to the pinnacles of the mountain ridges.

Behind, the hunters stalked, and ahead . . . he did not know what lay ahead. He simply stumbled on, pausing from time to time for breath, to try to wipe away the painful storm which raged within his deprived body.

The wind pressed him against the wall of stone rising to his left. The fringes on his buckskins whipped wildly in the wind. Ruff halted, leaning his head against the frozen stone. His eyes stared downward, red, raw, weary, and he noticed with numb disappointment that his rifle had dropped from his fingers. Sometime . . . unnoticed . . . lost . . .

Then from behind he heard a shout and he started on.

Below and a quarter of a mile behind, small dark figures wound their way along the twisting trail which led upward to where Ruff Justice waited. A wild, meaningless shot was fired upward, dying before it reached Ruff's feet.

Three men. And at their head—he knew it even at this distance—Roscoe Siringo. They rushed along the icy trail, and why not? They had Justice and they knew it.

Ruff knew it as well.

Turning his head again, he looked at the trail, which had crumbled away, leaving a fifty-foot-wide gap. And below lay stony death. This was it. The moment that had been endlessly forecast for him, the moment which had been retarded but never could be eluded. You walk into Death's arms and spit in his crooked face. You can manage it more than once with a little luck, a little confidence. But the old bastard grows angry with a man. And once you return without a supporting Fate standing at your shoulder, he'll turn, smiling all the while, and simply bite your head off.

Ruff could feel Death's hot breath above the cold wind.

Justice swung open the gate on his Colt and reloaded. Then he waited, watching the bend in the trail around which Siringo must come.

The clouds lowered their heads again and the snow began to fall. Justice hardly noticed it. All of his attention was focused on the bend in the trail. There, a wind-tormented pine, ancient and twisted, tilted out over the morass at his feet.

The darkness had begun to gray as dawn crept into the skies, the sun fizzling behind the banks of snow-laden clouds.

Ruff held his Colt inside his shirt, keeping it next to his body to prevent the action from freezing. Not that it would possibly matter. He was six left-handed shots away from eternity anyway. But perhaps one of those six bullets would find Siringo's black heart.

Would he bleed? Or was the bastard full of pus and bile? Maybe his blood had turned to silver.

The first man rounded the bend in the trail, and Ruff steadied himself, leaning against the cliff beside him as he brought his gun up left-handed. He triggered off, drawing an answering shot which rang off the stone beside Justice's head.

He fired again and saw the man drop his rifle, clasp his leg, and drag himself back around the bend. A second man appeared suddenly. This one, wearing a red mackintosh, flung himself to his belly and began levering .44s through his Henry repeater. Ruff turned away as the bullets, peppering the cliff, showered him with ice and rock splinters. His cheek stung and he felt blood trickling down to freeze against his face.

Jutice stood suddenly upright. If this was it, then goddammit, let them pay! He walked forward, his arm loose at his side, watching as the rifleman frantically shoveled fresh cartridges into the magazine of the Henry, his eyes wide and round above a black, matted beard.

"Ready?" Justice called out, and the calm in his voice seemed to panic the man. He steeled himself and jumped to his feet.

"You're damn right!"

Ruff nodded. "Then go to hell." He fired twice, seeing the snow on the front of the red mackintosh jump. The hired goon staggered backward and then was gone, his arms windmilling in the air as he dropped into the crevice, his death scream covered by the whine and whip of the wind.

Justice walked on, toward death, the snow frosting his hair, forming tiny icicles on his drooping mustache. The pain was gone, the caution, everything. Everything but the urge to kill, the driving need to take Roscoe Siringo with him into the black pit of a writhing, overcrowded hell.

Suddenly he was there. They faced each other across twenty feet of broken, snowy trail as the wind lifted Ruff's hair, as the lightning crackled across the void above and the thunder rumbled down the long canyons below.

He appeared from out of the mist and snow, rifle in his hands, and Ruff knew him. It was not so much that Siringo resembled the scratched and faded daguerreotype that Ruff carried, but that he looked at this man and saw no soul, no softness, only dirt and blood. Those eyes had never looked upon a loved one or fondly scanned a colorful sunrise. They had never counted the night stars, realizing how small and insignificant the man with the eyes was. They had seen the world only as a helpless thing to be raped and battered, a place to fill your pockets.

He had walked the earth killing because that

was the pleasure of life—to be able to end it for others.

It was there. In his eyes. And in the eyes of Ruff Justice at that moment, those cold blue eyes which had looked on this sort of bastard issue of a maddened Creation before, who had—eternally, it seemed—studied and tracked and killed this sort of scab, this sort of filth-encrusted, soulless replica of a man—in the eyes of Ruff, who had seen too many of these creatures, there was only the determination to stomp it, to kill it before it could harm more than it already had.

The loathing was deep and real and virulent, and Ruff had to slow his breathing, calm his heart. He had to be calm now, now when he had his chance, at the final moment.

Siringo continued to walk slowly forward, his jaw hanging open.

"Justice?" he finally said.

"That's right."

"I'm going to kill you."

He fired from the hip. No more conversation. Just Siringo moving in, firing with his Winchester as Ruff ducked and brought his Colt up.

Ruff felt searing pain low on his left side as if someone had jammed a red-hot branding iron against his flesh, and he was spun around, the Colt flying free. He heard the wind-roar, and above it the maddened howl of Siringo's laughter.

And then there was the other sound. Ruff, on his knees, holding his side, looked up to see Siringo standing over him, rifle leveled.

The growl was low, savage, rumbling, and Justice through the haze of pain saw what he *couldn't* have seen. He saw the flash of a body, felt the close brush of it, its heat, saw the eyes of Siringo open wide as the white wolf, half the size of a horse, launched itself toward his throat.

Siringo simply dropped his gun, screaming in terror, his hands going up protectively. But it was too late. The creature, the thing, the Windwolf, had him, and it mauled him savagely, shaking him as a pup shakes a rat, and Siringo's death scream died in his throat.

Justice tried to find his lost Colt revolver, he tried to rise, tried to make sense out of this, and failed. He sagged back to sit staring at the empty ledge, at the snow tumbling down from out of the frothing sky.

There was nothing there, nothing at all.

Siringo had gone over the ledge. His rifle still lay in the snow. Crawling forward, Justice looked over, seeing nothing but the snow washing through the gorge. There was no sign of Siringo.

Only a few drops of scarlet blood against the snow. And the massive wolf tracks.

17

The lean-to was small, clean, smelling of pine boughs. Ruff Justice opened his eyes and stared at the shelter, trying to organize the memories which swirled through his mind.

He recalled then staggering down the slope, someone calling to him. Then arms had been wrapped around him and he had been lifted onto a travois. There was that, and the woman leaning over him, her face intent, her eyes concerned.

There were other memories that made no sense. A wind-swept ledge, a massive white body, Siringo's mouth open in horror . . .

Ruff shook his head and tried to sit up. The pain shot through his side, and he lay back, dizzy and sick. His arm had been tightly bandaged, and now, feeling his ribs, he could see that some work had been done there as well.

How long had he been here? He looked outside and saw a miraculously blue sky, distant mountains. He was aware too of a ravenous hunger.

The shadow crossed his bed, and he looked up to see Dream Sky standing there. In her hand was a bowl.

"I thought you might be hungry," she said. "How do you feel?"

She bent low over Ruff, her long braids falling across his chest. His answer was to pull her down to him, to kiss her full, parting lips deeply, to hold her close—she who seemed real, alive, warm.

Her breath was warm against Ruff's chest as he stroked her hair. Dream Sky sat up, smiling.

"Your food."

"Later." Ruff smiled, and she nodded, rising to place a blanket across the lean-to opening before she shrugged out of the buckskin dress she wore and slipped in beside him, her breasts warm against his chest, her leg thrown up over his thigh.

She touched his side, and he winced. "Easy, girl," he said with a smile. "I'm badly damaged."

"Not where it matters, I think," Dream Sky said, and her fingers slid down across his belly to find Ruff, to encircle him.

The body which had seemed frozen, half dead, came to life, and as he responded to Dream Sky's touch she smiled, leaning forward to kiss his lips.

"Do nothing. Lie back, invalid. I shall do."

And she did; straddling him, she fitted them together, Ruff feeling the warm comfort of Dream Sky close around him. He stretched out his hands and fondled her breasts, his thumbs toying with her dark, taut nipples, as Dream Sky, a study in concentration, lifted her hips and worked her inner muscles against him.

She shuddered then and slowly lowered herself against him, her lips brushing his throat as her hips continued to convulse.

Dream Sky trembled in his arms. Her fingers searched his face, his shoulders, frantically, and she murmured, "It is good, Windwolf. It is good."

It was all of that. It was very good, and they loved the day away. Somewhere along the line Justice fell asleep, the girl snuggled in his arms. When he finally awakened she was gone, and he looked around, seeing the untouched bowl of food. Beyond the entranceway the sky was still blue, only small puffballs of white cloud floating over the mountains.

Justice struggled to a sitting position and finally, with a great effort, got to his feet. Finding his clothes, he dressed, moving carefully so as not to tear anything loose.

His gunbelt was there, but the holster was empty. He looked for his Spencer and found that it too was gone. He put on the gunbelt anyway and went out, ducking through the entrance to emerge into the brilliant sunlight. There children played. Faces turned toward him, smiling faces.

The sun was warm, the war gone from their home.

Stone Eyes appeared suddenly in front of him, rifle in hand, his face painted, his hair decorated with eagle feathers and red beads.

"I knew you would come out sometime," he said. His eyes were scathing, his voice a rumble deep in his throat. "Now we shall fight. Now I shall kill you."

Ruff, still weak from the loss of blood, peered at the blurred, wavering features of Stone Eyes. He shook his head.

"I don't understand, Stone Eyes."

"You understand me well enough. You ran away from us. There was a terrible battle. Ten men killed. While Windwolf hid in the forest."

Ruff nodded slowly, wearily. So that was what he thought—or was it? He suddenly saw through the words to the heart of the matter. It was Dream Sky. He had always been jealous of her love, this Ute warlord, and now he meant to kill Ruff over it.

"Stone Eyes!"

The voice belonged to Dream Sky. She ran, arms swinging, across the camp to where Ruff faced the Ute warrior. She stepped between them and slapped at Stone Eyes' chest with the flat of her hand.

"What is the matter with you? This is Windwolf! He who saved our people!"

"He is a white man. A liar and a fake," Stone Eyes said implacably. He tried to push Dream Sky away, but she clung to him, screaming.

"No! You cannot harm him! You cannot fight this man, Stone Eyes. He has only now risen from his sickbed."

"Then I shall wait. I shall wait and then I will kill him!"

Ruff was about to step in, to say something, but he caught the quick glance Dream Sky cast across her shoulder, a glance which was wise and deep, which revealed in that fragment of a second that she too knew what was at the bottom of Stone Eyes' hatred.

"Let this man go, my Stone Eyes," she said, her voice softening, her eyes pleading. She clung to his arms still, smiling up into the savage face of the Ute warlord. "What is he to us? We have each other, we have our home. This one"—she laughed, waving a hand in the air—"what is he? A white man, weak and stupid—why, he did not even know that I loved only you! He spoke to me with words of love. How could I listen, thinking of my Stone Eyes? You, my love, who must not be hurt."

"He cannot hurt me. Do you think I fear his false magic?"

"To kill him would mean more trouble, Stone Eyes," she persisted. "Perhaps white soldiers would come and then we must lose the peace you have fought for. Please, Stone Eyes! Please."

For a long minute Stone Eyes looked at Justice and then at the woman in his arms. Finally he replied.

"All right. For you I do this, Dream Sky. But he must go. Now! Injured or not. I will not have him here." He started to turn away, then halted. "Tomorrow," he said to the Ute woman. "Tomorrow we will be married. Make preparations."

Then he was gone, striding across the camp, the master of his world. Dream Sky turned silently toward Ruff, who smiled and nodded.

"Thank you."

She opened her mouth to answer, but she could not form the words. Tears clouded her eyes, and she wiped them away angrily. Ruff reached out for her, and she whirled away, running across the camp, the hot tears still stinging her eyes.

Justice turned, looking up toward the cloudless skies, the purple mountain peaks. Then he smiled. He stopped a small boy who was running past and said, "Do you know where my horse is, boy? Then get it."

It was still light when Justice rode out, although the shadows were deep at the foot of the mountains and the sky gradually purpling.

There was enough light so that he saw the woman standing in the grove of aspens, saw her damp eyes, the set expression on her beautiful face, saw Dream Sky lift a hand and hold it above

173

her shoulder for a moment before she turned and walked away, her arms folded.

Justice ached, body and mind. His head throbbed and he felt light-headed. His side ached, his shoulder nagged him painfully.

As he moved through the aspens and into the pine forest, the dark notch which was Frenchman's Pass above him, he began to whistle. After a time he grinned and rode on more quickly, the gray loping upward toward the high country.

And there was a time when the wild wind blew, as the mournful song keening through the pines took on an eerie tone, a satisfied, thrilling rumble as if a great Windwolf spoke from the heart of the mountains. Ruff Justice sat listening to it for a moment, and then he was gone, turning the gray toward Frenchman's, toward a world where legends did not take life and walk this earth, where things were a little simpler. And a little more empty.

WESTWARD HO!

The following is the opening chapter from the next novel in the gun-blazing, action-packed new Ruff Justice series from Signet:

RUFF JUSTICE #10: SHOSHONE RUN

The six men rested in the shifting shade of the cottonwoods looking out across the bright Dakota plains toward the sod-roofed house which sat beside the narrow creek. Five of the men wore army blue. The sixth, a tall, buckskin-clad man with long dark hair and a drooping mustache, was the civilian scout Ruffin T. Justice.

Justice squatted down, holding the reins to his black horse, squinting into the sunlight. A seventh soldier was returning on the double, running in a crouch, working his way through the willows along the creek.

"Hope to hell he's not down there," Corporal Todd Trent muttered. Justice glanced at Trent, a hatchet-faced man with dark eyes whose harsh features belied a somewhat gentle nature.

"He's down there," Ruff answered, rising, stretching his arms.

"How can you be so sure?" Trent asked, keeping his gaze on the soddy.

"Martha's there. This is where he always comes when he's drunk."

"Can't see what he sees in that sack of potatoes."

"She's a woman," Justice said, and Trent, lifting an eyebrow, nodded.

If Sergeant Walter Penrose, eighteen years' service, was down in that sod house, and Ruff felt sure he was, they could only hope he had managed to get himself dead drunk. Penrose was a hulking, powerful man with the mild disposition of a friendly sheepdog. When he was sober.

Unfortunately those times were few and far between these days, and Penrose drunk was an entirely different proposition. He had nearly destroyed the enlisted barracks at Fort Lincoln two weeks ago. A month before that he had wrecked a Bismarck saloon.

"The colonel's going to skin him this time," Trent said. "You know, Walt Penrose broke me in. He was a hell of a soldier. I don't understand what's happened to him. Oh . . . hell," Trent said in frustration.

To be accurate, the colonel wasn't going to skin Penrose; what he would do would be to bust him, and likely it would cost Penrose his pension. Justice got to his feet. The seventh soldier was coming in. His name was Schuyler, a likable red-faced kid who just now looked as worried as if he'd come upon a thousand of Red Cloud's Sioux warriors.

"He's down there," Schuyler reported breathlessly. "I seen his horse around back."

"Jesus," Trent sighed. The corporal looked around, straightening his hat. "Well, we got to go get him. Coming, Mr. Justice?"

Ruff only grinned. He wanted no part of Walt

Penrose just now. Trent smiled back feebly. "All right, boys, let's go fetch the sergeant."

Justice seated himself in the shade of a drooping cottonwood, knees drawn up, a blade of grass between his lips. Todd Trent, looking back, envied the man. Orders were orders. Justice's orders had been to find Walter Penrose. Trent's orders were to bring him in.

They approached the house on their horses, hoping there had been some kind of mistake, that Penrose wasn't inside. Corporal Trent swung down from his bay's back and walked to the door, which was of rough, weather-grayed planks. He knocked twice, heard some sort of hasty stirring within, and put his boot to the latch.

The door sprang open, and Trent had a glimpse of Big Martha—all three hundred pounds of her—running naked across the room, all of her tremendous body jiggling crazily, as she scampered for the back door.

In the bed lay Penrose, his whiskered jaw open, his snores echoing through the soddy. Trent glanced at Schuyler, the nearest soldier, and stepped forward to shake Penrose awake.

His hand closed around Sergeant Walt Penrose's massive arm, and the result was similar to touching a match to a keg of powder.

With a roar Penrose, dressed in red longjohns, smashed out with a meaty fist and leaped from the bed with an agility incredible for a man of his bulk. The fist caught Trent square in the face, and he was slammed back against the soddy's wall, his nose streaming blood.

He blinked away the bright, spinning dots and looked up in time to see Penrose pick up Schuyler

177

bodily and hurl him across the room to land on a rickety puncheon table, flattening it.

The soldiers moved in, and Penrose, a red-clad bear surrounded by angry blue hornets, struck out with lefts and rights, decking another man before Trent had staggered to his feet, rejoining the fray.

Things were going badly and it wasn't going to get much better, Trent decided. He took a soldier's Springfield rifle, gripped it by the barrel, and moved in, slamming the stock down against Penrose's neck at the base of the skull.

Penrose turned, holding his neck, blinked at Trent with sorrowful, blood-red eyes, and keeled over, landing with a heavy thump on the packed-earth floor.

"Take him out of here and tie him up," Trent panted, holding his handkerchief to his damaged nose to stanch the flow of blood. "No, wait! Tie him up and *then* take him out." It wouldn't do to have the bastard come around again.

Breathing curses, Trent picked up Sergeant Penrose's uniform, which was thrown into a corner of the room. His gunbelt and rifle were under the bed. Looking around, his nose wrinkling with disgust at the smell of the place, Trent went out, kicking the door shut.

Ruff Justice was leaning against his horse when the soldiers returned. Surveying the damage done, Ruff decided Penrose must have been asleep when they found him. Otherwise it would have been a hell of a lot worse.

The big man, still in longjohns, was trussed and thrown over the back of his horse. His head bobbed and rolled as they came up to where Ruff waited. Without warning Penrose opened his mouth and vomited all over the ground.

Then slowly the bleary eyes opened and he looked up. "Hello, Ruff," he said.

"Howdy, Walt. How's things?"

First Sergeant Mack Pierce stuck his head into the colonel's office and nodded. "They're coming in, sir."

"Fine." MacEnroe got to his feet, tugged his tunic down, and went out through the orderly room, squaring his hat as he moved.

The commanding officer of Fort Lincoln, Dakota Territory, stood on the plankwalk in front of the orderly room, watching as the outriders came in through the main gate. Behind them came the carriage itself, then two more riders.

MacEnroe stepped down into the cool sunlight as the carriage swung across the parade ground and drew up in a mist of fine dust.

The square-faced man with the iron-gray mustache stepped down first. He assisted the second passenger to the ground.

Colonel MacEnroe hadn't quite been prepared for this. The man turned and on his arm was the most astonishingly beautiful woman he had ever seen. Around twenty, the colonel guessed, with honey-blond hair piled attractively on a finely boned skull, she had a figure to take a man's breath away and weaken his knees. It was attractively presented in a pale-green and lace dress.

"Colonel MacEnroe?"

"Yes, sir," the colonel said a bit too sharply.

"Secretary McClellan," he said, sticking out a square red hand. "You received my wire?"

"Yes, sir." The colonel was still looking at the woman, who smiled back. The Secretary of the Interior's eyes narrowed and he said stiffly, "This is my wife, Angelique."

"Charmed," MacEnroe murmured. "Let's go into my office, shall we? I imagine you've had enough sun to last you. How was your journey?"

"Miserable," McClellan said bluntly.

"It was lovely," Angelique McClellan chirped, holding her husband's arm.

"Angelique's a maid of the West, you know," McClellan said as if apologizing. "She likes nothing more than riding across a hundred miles of empty treeless plains."

MacEnroe tried a smile which he hoped each would interpret as sympathy. Then he turned and extended an arm toward his orderly-room door. "Shall we?"

"Yes," Angelique McClellan said. "Polly, do come in with us, dear."

It was only then that MacEnroe noticed the second woman. She still sat beside the driver of the carriage, a small, quite young girl with dark hair severely arranged. She wore a trim gray suit and a tiny gray hat.

"My companion, Polly," Angelique said. The girl was helped down and introduced to Colonel MacEnroe. Then they entered the headquarters building, Mack Pierce following them. The sergeant had somewhere found tea and a china serving set, and he placed it on the colonel's desk, smiling at the ladies.

Angelique responded with a melting smile. Polly sat stiffly in a wooden chair, hands tightly clasped. MacEnroe produced a bottle of whiskey, and John McClellan, rubbing his hands together, accepted a glass.

MacEnroe watched the man, seeing only steel and leather. McClellan was a hard one, had always been. Colonel MacEnroe knew all about McClellan, although their paths had never crossed before.

McClellan had been a soldier. Out of Pennsylvania he had been a brevet colonel under General John Pope and had distinguished himself at Cedar Mountain against Jackson. Later he had been attached to Grant's staff, and he had ridden Grant's coattails to Washington, accepting the appointment of Secretary of the Interior, a post for which he was no more qualified than Grant was to be President, but which he administered ruthlessly. Incredibly, this was McClellan's first trip west.

The Secretary explained: "Congress thought it was time to take a real look at this western territory, to plan for its future beyond the time when the Indians are defeated, as they must inevitably be."

MacEnroe lifted an eyebrow. "At times out here, sir, it doesn't seem all that inevitable."

"It's a matter of numbers and organization, colonel. All war is a matter of numbers. Numbers of soldiers, numbers of weapons. In that sense might is right, as has been said; the only real strength is the strength of arms."

"I suppose," MacEnroe muttered.

"At any rate, I'm out here to look over the country. They're talking about raising wheat in this country." McClellan shook his head at the stupidity of some people. "Great cities, they say, will sprout up on these plains. I remain skeptical.

181

However, there is a meeting next week in Fargo. The Agriculture Secretary will be there, someone from War—General Briggs, I believe—and several local bigwigs. At that meeting suggestions and recommendations for the future development of Dakota Territory will be mapped out. I will then make my report to the Congress."

MacEnroe nodded. Rising, he poured tea for Angelique McClellan and then for the silent companion girl.

"Mrs. McClellan, as I understand it, will not be going on to Fargo?"

"No. My wife is a foreigner, you know," the Secretary said with a hint of a smile. "One of these Canucks. Raised in Saskatchewan near . . ."

"Oxbow, darling," Angelique said, her eyes sparkling. God, what a woman, MacEnroe thought enviously. How did a prig like McClellan ever land her?

"Oxbow, which as I understand is just over the Canadian line. Angelique has not been home for a long while, and she wishes to take this opportunity to see friends in Oxbow. I have therefore requested that the army provide her with an escort to the Canadian line. There a contingent of the Saskatchewan Internal Security forces will see her safely to Oxbow."

"You have family there still, Mrs. McClellan?" the colonel asked.

"Unfortunately, no. Mother died years ago, and my father was killed by Ojibwa Indians just after the war. That was when I came south to live with an aunt in Philadelphia—where I met my charming young soldier."

She smiled at McClellan, who took her hand.

182

"Angelique will have two weeks while I wrap up my affairs at Fargo. What is the Indian situation, colonel?"

"Not good." MacEnroe leaned back in his chair. "However, it has been much worse. I should think that we can provide adequate protection. All reports are that the Sioux have drifted south with the arrival of spring."

"I can't tell you how important Angelique is to me," the Secretary said, and there was hidden menace in his voice.

"I quite understand, sir," the colonel said quickly. "Every precaution will be taken. I will use a contingent of my best men."

"You have someone who knows that country?"

"Yes, sir." MacEnroe frowned slightly. "I have someone who knows it very well."

The companion girl, who had been sitting silent with hands wrapped around her teacup, suddenly blurted out: "Sir, if it is at all possible—I have a request to make of you, sir."

"A request?" MacEnroe smiled at Polly. The girl looked so small and defenseless. She was flushed now and trembling. It must have taken a great effort for her to speak up.

"Yes, sir. If it is at all possible, I would like to ask for a particular man to be assigned to this detail."

"You know one of my men?"

"Yes, sir. Well, that is I *don't* know him. But I would like to very much." She paused and licked her dry lips. "I would like to request that Sergeant Walter Penrose be assigned to our party."

"Penrose!" MacEnroe couldn't suppress the small explosion. That drunken reprobate, a disgrace to his uniform. He was glad, a moment later, that he had said none of that out loud.

"Yes, sir. You see—Sergeant Walter Penrose is my father."

MacEnroe was stunned into immobility. He caught the Secretary's hard, curious glare on him. "Is there something wrong, colonel? Is there some reason this simple request cannot be fulfilled?"

"No, sir," MacEnroe said quickly. "None at all. I was only surprised to discover that Sergeant Penrose had a daughter."

"It's the reason Polly decided to come west with me," Angelique McClellan put in. She reached over and patted Polly's hand. "She hasn't seen her father since she was very young. In a way, you see, this is a homecoming for both of us. I'm returning to visit Canada, and Polly—she's come to see her father."

"Yes." MacEnroe smiled. He was standing near the window now. From there he could see directly across parade to the guardhouse. "Very well," he agreed. "We will see that Sergeant Penrose is assigned to this detail."

If we can get him on his feet.

"Justice?"

Ruff looked up from his bunk, where he sat repairing his saddlebags. The corporal grinned and nodded toward the headquarters building.

"What is it, Bill?"

"The colonel wants to see you." The corporal winked. "And you won't be sorry you went."

The door was pulled shut, and Ruff Justice got lazily to his feet, putting his saddlebags aside. He walked to the smoky mirror, swept back his long dark hair, and yawned.

Planting his hat, he went through the door himself, striding across the parade ground, where a squad of soldiers going through mounted drill was stirring up clouds of cinnamon-colored dust.

First Sergeant Mack Pierce was behind his desk, sleeves rolled up, attacking a mountain of paperwork. He glanced up as Justice entered.

"Go on in, Ruff."

Justice did so. He stepped into the colonel's office, finding MacEnroe at his desk, a tall strong-looking man standing at the window, and across the room in a wooden chair, holding a dainty teacup between smooth white hands, a dazzling honey blonde with flashing eyes.

Ruff smiled and nodded, and she beamed in answer. If that wasn't an invitation, or at least deep curiosity, Justice had never seen an invitation in a woman's eyes.

The colonel cleared his throat, and Justice turned toward him. "Secretary McClellan, may I present the man who will be in charge of this expedition. Ruffin T. Justice."

JOIN THE <u>RUFF JUSTICE</u> READER'S PANEL
AND PREVIEW NEW BOOKS

If you're a reader of <u>RUFF JUSTICE</u>, New American Library wants to bring you more of the type of books you enjoy. For this reason we're asking you to join <u>RUFF JUSTICE</u> Reader's Panel, to preview new books, so we can learn more about your reading tastes.

Please fill out and mail today. Your comments are appreciated.

1. The title of the last paperback book I bought was: _____

2. How many paperback books have you bought for yourself in the last six months?
☐ 1 to 3   ☐ 4 to 6   ☐ 10 to 20   ☐ 21 or more

3. What other paperback fiction have you read in the past six months?
Please list titles: _____

4. I usually buy my books at: (Check One or more)
☐ Book Store   ☐ Newsstand   ☐ Discount Store
☐ Supermarket   ☐ Drug Store   ☐ Department Store
☐ Other (Please specify) _____

5. I listen to radio regularly: (Check One)   ☐ Yes   ☐ No
My favorite station is: _____
I usually listen to radio (Circle One or more)   On way to work /
During the day / Coming home from work / In the evening

6. I read magazines regularly: (Check One)   ☐ Yes   ☐ No
My favorite magazine is: _____

7. I read a newspaper regularly: (Check One)   ☐ Yes   ☐ No
My favorite newspaper is: _____
My favorite section of the newspaper is: _____

For our records, we need this information from all our Reader's Panel Members.
NAME: _____
ADDRESS: _____ ZIP _____
TELEPHONE: Area Code ( ) Number _____

8. (Check One)   ☐ Male   ☐ Female

9. Age (Check One)   ☐ 17 and under   ☐ 18 to 34
☐ 35 to 49   ☐ 50 to 64   ☐ 65 and over

10. Education (Check One)
☐ Now in high school   ☐ Graduated high school
☐ Now in college   ☐ Completed some college
☐ Graduated college

As our special thanks to all members of our Reader's Panel, we'll send a free gift of special interest to readers of <u>RUFF JUSTICE</u>.

Thank you. Please mail this in today.

NEW AMERICAN LIBRARY
PROMOTION DEPARTMENT
1633 BROADWAY
NEW YORK, NY 10019